DREAD WOOD

For Les Hall, who props me up with her unwavering support and kindness. And for Taylor Swift, who inspires me with the perfect words and beautiful worlds she writes.

First published in Great Britain in 2022 by Farshore
An imprint of HarperCollins*Publishers*
1 London Bridge Street, London SE1 9GF

farshore.co.uk

HarperCollins*Publishers*
1st Floor, Watermarque Building, Ringsend Road
Dublin 4, Ireland

Text copyright © Jennifer Killick 2022
Illustration copyright © Tom Clohosy Cole 2022

The moral rights of the author and illustrator have been asserted

ISBN 978 0 7555 0371 1

Printed and bound in the UK using 100% renewable electricity at
CPI Group (UK) Ltd

1

A CIP catalogue record for this title is available from the British Library.

MIX
Paper from
responsible sources
FSC™ C007454

JENNIFER KILLICK

DREAD WOOD

Farshore

CHAPTER ONE

CLUB LOSER

There aren't many worse things than being in school, but being in school on a Saturday is one of them. Water drips off the trees that loom like ancient sentinels over the path to the locked gates, and circle the grounds all the way to the Dread Wood that backs on to the school. I wonder how many weekend detentions they've watched over. How many groups of hacked-off kids scuffing up the gravel lane, wishing they were somewhere else. An icy droplet falls from a low oak branch, rolls down my neck and under the collar of my sweatshirt, but I see the others – three of them – waiting up ahead, so I make sure I don't flinch. When I reach the gates I keep my head down so I won't make eye contact.

'I'd honestly rather be dead than here right now,' Hallie says. I know it's her without looking up because it's the kind of stupid thing she'd say.

'Really?' someone snorts. It's Gus, the crazy kid who seems to live his life by a different set of rules to everyone else. I have no idea what they are – he's as unpredictable as a dog in a field of squirrels. Like walking chaos. 'This is a seriously grim way to spend a Saturday, but I'm not sure it's as bad as death.'

'Of course it isn't,' the other girl snaps. Naira. Uptight, overachiever, one hundred per cent perfect, on the surface. Spends a lot of her time using her brilliance to make other people feel worthless. 'And, let me make it clear right now that none of you are to talk to me for the duration of this consequence. I don't want anything to do with any of you losers.'

Gus laughs.

'If we're losers, Naira,' Hallie says, 'then welcome to the club.'

'Club Loser!' Gus whoops, jumping up and grabbing a tree branch, sending a shower of water drops over everyone else. He swings there for a few seconds, as Naira shrieks and Hallie swears, both of them swiping at the droplets like they're being stung by wasps.

I let the water roll down my face, enjoying the thought that it's been on an epic journey, falling from the clouds high above, then trickling through the tree, and finally landing on me. I look up at Gus.

'We should make a badge, guys,' he shouts. 'I'll use my best pens to draw a logo. And we simply *must* have a motto.' He puts on a fake posh voice for the last part.

'Have some respect for the tree, lame-brain,'

Hallie says. 'It's like a million years old. If you break that branch, I'll break your arm.' Hallie uses her anger for both good and evil – it seems to me she has a ton of it stored up and she loudly puts it on display. There are unauthorised pin badges on her sweatshirt declaring her pride in being vegetarian, an LGBTQ+ ally, and a welcomer of refugees.

'It's just a dirty lump of wood and dry leaves,' says Naira, glaring upwards while smoothing her hair back.

'I know we're not friends, but describing me like that is hurtful, Naira.' Gus drops from the branch, and I let out a snort of laughter, even though I hadn't planned to.

'So he is listening,' Hallie says, hands on her hips like she's just won a game.

Gus's eyes open wide and he clutches Hallie's arm. 'Wait. Do trees have ears?'

'She meant Loner Boy over there.' Naira tilts her head in my direction. 'Table-flipper.'

'Yeah, all right, tray-launcher,' I say. 'I seem

to remember it was you who started the whole thing.' I regret speaking as soon as the words are out of my mouth. Just like I regret lasting less than three months in Year 7 before getting involved in a situation that the rest of the school now refers to as 'The Dread Wood Riot'. Riot is an exaggeration, but I can see how it led to all of us being here, in detention, on a Saturday. Anyway, let the rest of them think what they want, and don't get involved. I just have to get through the next four hours.

The sound of someone whistling makes me turn back to the gates. The school groundskeeper is walking slowly towards us, keys dangling.

'Finally,' Naira says. 'Let us in, will you, so we can get this over with?'

'Someone's in a hurry.' He smiles as he chooses a key from the bunch and puts it into the lock.

'She knows she's here for the same reason as the rest of us, right?' Gus whispers to Hallie, loud enough so we can all hear.

'Not sure,' Hallie says. 'You can never tell with Naira. I don't think anyone really knows her.'

'Is her name even Naira?' Gus whispers as we start to crunch up the drive. Naira is speeding ahead, Gus a few metres behind her, talking to himself, with Hallie trailing, eyes glued to the phone in her hand. I keep to the back, still in half a mind to turn and run. I notice a beetle on my sleeve that must have fallen with the rainwater from the tree. I let it crawl on to my finger, then carefully transfer it back to the trunk of the nearest oak. As it stops to take in its surroundings, I hear the school gates clank shut behind me, and the click as the groundskeeper locks us in. The moment for escape has gone.

'You're to sign in at student services,' the groundsman calls. 'Mr Canton will meet you there. Good luck.' He starts whistling again – sharp and clear. It's a familiar tune that I can't quite place and I can't be bothered to wonder about. None of us turn around and thank him.

Dread Wood High is a weird place – a mix of old and new, historical and modern, in the way it looks and the way it feels. The main reception and offices are in the old mansion, a grand building that would be nice to look at if it wasn't a school. Imagine horses pulling carriages, ladies in bonnets, and gentlemen in high boots and frilly shirts, and you'll get the picture. It has a conservatory and ornamental gardens out the back, but only sixth formers and teachers are allowed in there. Nothing makes me want to see a place more than being told I'm not allowed, but when I sneaked on to the science-block roof once, I got a good look. There are bushes cut into ball shapes, a pond with a fountain, and a load of smug Year 12s, who didn't notice me laughing at them. I'm not bothered about going in there now. It's the kind of place where, if it was in a movie, there would either be a wedding or a murder. You'd think they would have used a place like this for something nice, but I guess whoever owned it was some kind of charity do-gooder because instead they decided to turn it into a school for the local estate kids.

The rest of the school was added bit by bit as they took on more kids, so every building is in its own different style. None of it matches or connects. Even more random is that when the school was a rich person's manor they kept animals on the land, and the school kept them on. I mean, obviously the original animals died a long time ago, but they still keep pigs and chickens for 'student well-being'. The pig yard is my favourite place in the school.

Student services is downstairs in the main classroom block – a concrete place that looks like a prison or hospital from the outside. Not much difference, really, as I want to be there as much as I'd want to be in either of those places. When we arrive, Mr Canton is waiting. We were told to wear our PE kits and trainers for 'outdoor activities' – no further explanation given – and Mr Canton is dressed in a painfully neat, matching tracksuit, T-shirt and middle-aged trainers that he clearly thinks are cool, but are not. He has a baseball cap and clipboard in his hand.

'Good morning, Mr Canton.' Naira smiles. Putting on the perfection again. 'I'm so sorry you had to give up your Saturday morning to oversee our totally justified Back On Track session.'

'Morning, guys! Great day for it,' he bounces as he talks.

'Are we going out on your yacht?' Gus asks, in a posh voice to copy Mr Canton's. 'Or perhaps a spot of lacrosse?'

I bite my lip so I don't laugh. I am not here to get pally with anyone, even though Gus is proving to be entertaining. School is a place I come to as little as I can get away with. It's pointless, just a waste of time when I could be earning money to help my family. And no one else at Dread Wood High can understand that. I've tried having friends in the past, and it just ends in a mess, so there's no way I'm going to waste my time buddying up with this lot.

'L-O-L!' Mr Canton smiles, and we all visibly cringe. Even Naira's fake smile cracks. 'By the end of today's session, I'm sure you'll all be right back on track and heading towards greatness.' He puts his hand up to shield his eyes like he's looking off into the distance.

'Or we'll be considering throwing ourselves on the track,' Hallie says.

'Come on, Hallie. Let's see that positive mental attitude. I know it's in there somewhere.' He ticks off our names on his clipboard list.

'What's with the Victorian register?' Gus says. 'Are you sending us to clean the chimneys? Are we doing role play? Oh, should I get changed?'

'Excellent questions, Mister Gustav,' Mr Canton chuckles. 'And as much as I'd like to train you up to be a gang of raggedy pickpockets, I'm afraid that's not on the agenda for today. We're having some technical difficulties, hence the return to paper and pen.'

Did he just say hence?

'You just said hence,' Hallie groans.

'Personally, I'm grateful for the opportunity to realign my vision and values, sir,' says Naira.

'That's the spirit.' He grins. 'And how about you, Angelo?' He turns to me. 'Are you ready to start turning things around? Hashtag "get things Back On Track"?'

Mr Canton is actually all right, but he clearly needs help.

'Sir,' I say. 'No one hashtags any more.'

'What? I thought it was all the rage on the socials.'

'No, Mr C,' Hallie says. 'Just no.'

'Right then,' he says. 'Onwards!' And he marches out of student services like this is his best day ever. We follow him past the main block and over to the tennis courts. A pale sun dips in and out of scurrying clouds, sending shafts of weak sunshine across the flat grey expanse. He opens the PE locker – which is basically a big shed next to the courts – and pulls out some black bags and litter pickers.

'Bags inside the locker, please,' he gestures for us to put our stuff inside. 'They'll be safe in here. Plus . . .' he straps a pouch that matches his tracksuit around his waist and unzips it, 'I'll take your phones.'

We all groan.

'Mr C, my phone does not want to be anywhere near your bumbag.' Hallie looks at the pouch in disgust. 'Seriously, I'd rather set it on fire.'

'They'll be safe in here,' he grins. 'I promise to protect them with my life.'

'I don't have a phone,' Gus says. 'I'm off grid right now.'

'Hand it over, Gustav,' Mr Canton says. 'And make sure you turn them off. I don't want any startling vibrations going off in my man pouch.'

Naira sighs and hands him her phone. Gus pulls his out of his pocket, switches it off and passes it over. I know there's no point arguing so I hand mine in too. Hallie clings to hers, looking like she's going to be sick.

'Hallie,' Mr Canton says. 'Come on.'

'This is an infringement of my human rights.'

'It's just a phone.'

'This is like a punishment from the Dark Ages – I'm sure there are laws against taking someone's phone at the weekend.'

'In case you've forgotten, you're here for a reason, Hallie. This is a Back On Track session – a consequence, not a punishment. Let's grab this opportunity to remind ourselves of our school values. TRACK: what does it stand for?'

We all look at him, eyes rolling.

'Angelo.' He turns to me. 'Let's start with you. The "T" in TRACK, what value does it correspond to?'

'Teamwork,' I say.

'And Gustav, give me the "R", please.'

Gus opens his mouth to speak.

'And let's not waste time going through all the negative "R" words you know – rubbish, ridiculous, ramshackle. I've heard them all before.'

'If those are the bad "R" words you've heard, sir, I really think I could blow your mind with some new vocab.' Gus grins.

'Just the value, please, Gus,' Mr Canton says.

Gus sighs. 'Respect.'

'And Hallie, what's the "A", please?'

Hallie smiles. 'Authoritarianism?'

Mr Canton smiles back. 'While I am very impressed by your vocabulary, Hallie, that was not the word I was looking for. Here's a clue – this word is particularly relevant to you.'

'Can I guess?' Gus raises his hand. 'A bunch of words come to mind.'

Hallie stink-eyes Gus and sighs. '"A" is for Attitude.'

'Excellent, I knew it was in there somewhere,'

says Mr Canton. 'Definitely one for you to mull over, Hallie, while your phone is safe in my man pouch.'

He holds his hand out. Hallie huffs and swears, and finally hands over her phone.

'The good news is that I think you all have plenty of value "C" – Curiosity – already, so let's move to . . .'

'"K" is for Kindness,' Naira butts in.

'Great enthusiasm there, Naira,' says Mr C. 'Lovely to see you keen as always, but what I want you to do is really think about that word, what it means, and how you put it into action.'

I've known Naira since primary. She's the star pupil, perfect scores in everything, and works harder than anyone. This is the first time I've ever seen her get in trouble. But for all that perfection, she doesn't seem happy. It's been a long time since I saw a genuine smile on her face.

'I'm kind,' Naira says. She might as well have said 'I'm purple' or 'I'm Batman', and it would have been as true. Everyone makes a face. 'What? I am! I organise fundraising events, I help at the senior citizen coffee mornings, I did a flipping sponsored silence for orphaned elephants, for flip's sake. Why would I do those things if I wasn't kind?'

'So you could get elected to the student council,' Hallie says.

'So you can write it on your university application,' I add, seeing as she asked.

'Because you love the smell of old people's hair,' says Gus. 'Every time you lean over to give them a refill, you get to inhale that fossilised goodness.'

'We're not here to cast judgements, guys,' Mr C says, giving us a look. 'But what I'd like you to think about, Naira, is motivation. If you do something kind because it will benefit you in some way, is it really kindness?'

Naira opens her mouth, but can't seem to find the words. As unlikely as it is, I swear she looks hurt.

'About my phone,' Hallie says, and the rest of us groan. 'What if there's an emergency?'

'We're in school for a few hours to see if we can get you guys working together and hashtag "Back On Track". We're going to be collecting litter, tending to the school animals, and hopefully having some first-class bantz . . .'

Another group groan.

'. . . nothing even remotely bad is going to happen.'

And then a noise rings out – a desperate scream that splits the quiet of the empty grounds and fills the air around us. It's like nothing I've ever heard before and a sound I know I'll never unhear. It's urgent fear and pain. And it's coming from inside the grounds.

CHAPTER TWO

TRACK

'Stay here,' Mr Canton says, putting the litter-picking stuff on the ground. 'I mean it – nobody move from this spot.'

He jogs across the tennis courts towards the field.

We look at each other for a second. No one says anything, but at the same moment, we all turn to follow him, running fast to catch up. The scream was harrowing, but at this point I'm more curious than scared.

'What the hell was that?' Hallie asks, her cheeks pink from the cold.

'School ghost,' Gus says. 'Everyone knows Dread Wood High is haunted. There are tons of stories about people hearing weird noises in the walls, and seeing spooky lights in the windows at night, when no one's supposed to be here.'

'The ghost, which doesn't exist by the way,' says Naira, 'is supposed to haunt the mansion, not the field.'

'Maybe it likes to go for a run on Saturdays.' Gus is starting to get out of breath. 'Just because you're dead, it doesn't mean you shouldn't be buff.'

'I'm eighty per cent sure it was an animal,' I say, my eyes sweeping the field ahead. 'Probably one of the pigs.'

'I have never heard an animal make a sound like that,' Hallie huffs.

'Yeah, Angelo, pigs oink, not scream. We learned that in nursery,' says Gus.

Naira is gliding along like a pro, not even breathing heavy yet. 'Angelo was probably out

19

stealing cars when we were in nursery.'

I ignore her and try to ignore the sting her comment has left. Naira knows me better than anyone else here, and while I can understand why most of the Dread Wood kids assume stuff about me, the judgement feels harsh coming from her.

Mr Canton has stopped in front of the pig yard, and he's crouching down to look at something on the ground.

'What is it, sir?' Hallie says.

'I told you all to stay put.' He turns and frowns at us.

We ignore him and gather around to look at what he's found in the grass. There's a substance attached to a clump of dandelions – white but with a transparency to it, thin and light, blowing in the wind like a flap of dead skin.

'Don't touch it,' Mr Canton says, poking it with a stick.

The grass around it has been flattened, but is otherwise undamaged, so whatever the white stuff is, I don't think it's harmful. I reach out and give it a gentle pull, expecting it to tear easily. It doesn't.

'Angelo, I said not to touch it,' Mr Canton sighs.

'What is it, Angelo?' Gus asks. 'Looks kinda like dried glue.'

'It's sticky,' I say, rubbing it between my fingers. 'And strong.'

'Ghost residue,' Gus nods.

'But what made the noise?' Hallie says. ''Cos I don't think it was that white ick.'

I look at the area where the grass is flat. There are drag marks in the earth, like something heavy was pulled along the ground. 'Where are the pigs?'

'OMG, the pigs,' Hallie gasps.

'Right.' Mr Canton stands up and faces us. 'This is not exactly how I anticipated our session going, but let's turn it to our advantage and use it to work on our values. I want to see excellent communication and teamwork while we go and check on the pigs, who I'm sure are absolutely fine, and happy as pigs in the proverbial.' He laughs and looks round at all of us like we should be laughing too, but we all just stare back. 'Come on then,' he says.

We walk across the yard to the stone building where the school's well-being pigs are kept. There are five of them – Gloucestershire Old Spots – pink with black patches, and ears that flop forward. They're usually snuffling around the yard at this time of day, but there's no sign of them as we approach. The building is L-shaped, with two pig enclosures in the main part, and a storage area where the animal and gardening supplies are kept – straw, buckets, that kind of stuff. The groundskeeper's ride-on lawnmower is parked outside as usual. It's like a mini tractor slash quad bike, with cutting blades. I've promised myself that I'm going to bomb round the field on it one day. The teachers say it's good to have ambitions.

'I'll look in on them,' Mr Canton says. 'You guys stay behind me.'

Hallie, Gus and I run forward to get to the opening first, and I don't know what we're expecting to find. It takes my eyes a moment to adjust to the gloom, and then I make out the pigs huddled together in the far corner.

'Ugh, they're fine,' Gus says. 'What an anticlimax.'

'They're not,' I say. 'They're agitated. Look how restless they are, and jumpy.' I like the pigs – I spend a fair bit of time here during breaks.

'And there are only four.' Hallie points. 'One of them is missing.'

'Are you sure?' Mr Canton comes puffing up behind us.

'I might not be in the top group for maths, but I can count to five,' Hallie says.

Dread Wood has two adult pigs, fat and friendly, and three piglets who – and I wouldn't use this expression out loud – are super cute.

'Arabella is missing,' I say.

'You know the pigs' names?' Naira's behind

me, so I can't see her face, but she sounds genuinely surprised, and not like she's being snaky.

'Yeah. There's one for each value – Theodora and Reggie are the big ones, and the piglets are Arabella, Candice and Klaus.'

'But how can you tell which is which? They all look the same.'

'That is so offensive, Naira,' Hallie huffs. 'Every pig is unique, like humans. Arabella has a heart-shaped black patch on her belly.'

'And she squeaks when you scratch behind her ears,' I add.

'Yeah, and pigs have feelings too,' Gus snorts. 'Remember your kindness-training, Naira.'

'Guys, let's focus,' Mr Canton says. 'We're going to work in teams. Angelo and Hallie, you're both familiar with the pigs, so I want you to feed and settle them. Naira and Gus, I want you to start searching the field for Arabella. I'm going to see Mr Latchitt to let him know we have a missing pig on our hands.'

'Would that be Mr Latchitt, the famous private investigator?' Gus says. 'Are we going to hire him? Do you need us all to help with his fee? I have twenty-three pence that I'd be willing, nay, happy to contribute.'

'Mr Latchitt is the groundskeeper. You walk past him every day. He let you into school this morning.'

'Oh, the whistling guy,' Hallie says.

'Honestly, you kids,' Mr Canton says. 'In a world of your own. Right, we all have our tasks – let's get going.'

Mr Canton, Naira and Gus jog off, leaving me, Hallie, the pigs and an awkward silence. I'm surprised when Hallie goes straight over to the pigs and crouches down to pat them and scratch the backs of their heads.

'What happened, guys?' she asks. 'Are you OK?'

Theodora and Reggie are standing protectively in front of Candice and Klaus, who are squeaking and shaky on their legs. They're all classic pig pink, but with black spots in different patterns, so they're easy to tell apart. Theo and Reg are enormous, but gentle unless they think the piglets are being threatened, and the piglets are young enough to be sweet and playful, but old enough to have developed their own personalities. Arabella's the most confident one, always a couple of steps ahead of the others. Candice looks like she's smiling all the time and wiggles her bum when she plays in the yard. Klaus is my favourite – when he looks into your eyes, it's like he's staring into your soul. Like he just gets it.

'We should check them over,' I say. 'Make sure they're not hurt.'

'Good idea,' says Hallie. 'Shall I keep them calm while you take a look?'

I nod and crouch next to her, ready to back off if Reg and Theo object to us handling the babies, but they're all right with us, and let me run my hands over them looking for injuries while Hallie chats to them and rubs their backs.

They're covered in pale, soft hairs that I smooth down as I examine them. I give Klaus an extra cuddle to reassure him, making sure to make eye contact and give him a nod. 'You're OK now,' I say.

I turn to Hallie. 'No injuries that I can make out. I think they're just scared.'

'If I had my phone, I'd play them some music,' Hallie says, putting her hand in her pocket, just in case it's somehow magicked its way there. 'They always like that.'

'You know each other,' I say, because it's clear that Hallie's spent some time here.

'I go to animal welfare club,' she says. 'I like being with the school animals, especially these guys – I love them so much. They make me feel calm. I've not seen you here though, after school.'

'I come here at other times. Breaks, PE, English, maths . . .'

Hallie laughs. 'You should join animal welfare club – you'd love it.'

'I always have to get home,' I say. 'Stuff to do.'

'Like what?' she says, looking across at me.

I hesitate before answering. I don't like telling people things about my life, but I know Hallie's like an anaconda wrapped around a deer – she'll just keep squeezing till I cave in. 'My parents both work a lot. I take care of my brother, do jobs around the estate to make extra money.'

'I didn't know that,' she says.

I shrug. 'We should sort the pigs out. You want to feed or muck out?'

'Literally nobody is going to choose shovelling pig poo over pouring food in a trough,' Hallie says, standing up.

I stand up too. 'I don't actually mind it. I find the smell comforting.'

'Even Reggie's giant piles of poo?'

'Yeah, even those.' I smile.

We walk out to the storage shed and collect the things we need. I'm thinking how surprised

I am to discover that Hallie is actually not that bad. I wonder if she's thinking the same thing about me. Then I lose myself in the scrape of my spade on the stone floor, and spreading clean straw until Naira and Gus come running into the sty, freaking out the pigs who we'd finally calmed down.

'Has Mr Canton been here?' Naira says, looking more stressed out than I've ever seen, aside from earlier this week in the dining hall.

'Nope,' I say. 'You found Arabella?'

'Not only have we not found Arabella,' Gus pants, 'but we've lost Mr C.'

Hallie looks up from the piglets. 'How do you lose Mr C? He's *always* there whether you like it or not. Like your alarm on Monday morning, or gum stuck under the desk.'

'He said he'd meet us in the new quad in fifteen minutes, but he didn't show,' Naira says. 'We waited thirty minutes, freezing our butts off, then went looking for him.'

'I thought he'd probably gone for a sneaky

dump, so we went to the staff room in the mansion, cos that's where I'd go if I needed a sneaky dump . . .'

'And what we found were signs of a disturbance, and this . . .' Naira shoves Mr C's cap at us.

'He probably just put it down and forgot about it,' Hallie says.

'Nah.' Gus shakes his head. 'It was on the floor by an overturned table and a mess of other stuff. And unless Angelo lost his shiz again and re-enacted the Great Dining Hall Table Flip of November the twentieth, something else knocked the stuff over, and did something to Mr C.'

'So now we're missing a pig and a teacher,' Naira huffs. 'Which is unlikely to be a coincidence.'

'We should look for them, right?' Hallie says.

'Sounds like a job for Club Loser!' Gus shouts. 'Do we have time to whizz up some costumes?'

'No costumes,' Naira says. 'No messing

around, and no splitting up. We'll look for them together.'

Hallie stands and dusts the grit from her hands. 'Where should we start?'

I stand next to Hallie. 'Mr Canton said he was going to see the groundskeeper – Mr Latchitt.' The whistling man. 'We should start there.'

CHAPTER THREE

EYE SPY

The groundskeeper and his wife live in a cottage next to the school, in a fenced-off area that backs on to the train tracks. Mrs Latchitt is a tiny lady, who seems to get smaller and more frail every time I see her – she looks like a withered-up baby bird that won't survive the winter. I'm not sure exactly what her job at the school is, but I sometimes see her being busy in the school kitchens. To be honest, she looks too fragile to do much at all.

Mr Latchitt is a big man, who I've never paid much attention to. He's a background person

– often there without you much noticing, mopping up a spill, carrying boxes or working with the pigs or random animals in the creature corner of the science block. When I try to picture him in my head, I can't recall his face. He's stored in my brain as a lurking figure wearing a muddle of different dark colours. And always with the whistle.

'We should be careful,' I say, as I turn from the pig yard to see a spiral of wood smoke rising above the trees across the Dread Wood.

'Of a couple of pensioners?' Gus says. 'In case they invite us in for tea and out-of-date biscuits?'

'Mr Canton disappeared when he went to look for Mr Latchitt,' I say. 'And I don't know much about them. Do any of you?'

'I only found out they existed this morning,' says Hallie. 'So I've got nothing.'

'She's the woman who helps in the dining hall and science labs sometimes, right?' Gus says. 'The one who looks close to death?'

'She's harmless, surely,' Naira says. 'I don't see how she could be a threat.'

'She might be a sniper, though,' Gus says. 'And Mr Latchitt is like half man, half bear. He'd destroy almost anyone in a fight.'

'I'm not saying they've done anything. I'm just saying that as we don't know what happened, we should approach with caution. Maybe try to stake out the place before we knock on the door.'

'And who exactly put you in charge?' Naira snaps.

I ignore it. 'I'm going round the back of their house to have a look first. You can do what you like.' And I walk off before there's any more discussion.

'Wait up.' Hallie comes jogging after me. 'I'm coming with you.'

After a few seconds Gus joins us and then I hear Naira fall in behind. I don't know if I'm relieved or annoyed that they're following.

We make our way across the wilder part

of the field behind the science block, and then cross the expanse of grass that leads to the fence around the Latchitts' cottage. Their front gate faces the school car park, so I avoid that and skirt the ivy-covered fence the opposite way, keeping close so that I won't be seen from the house. The others do the same, though they're not exactly inconspicuous. I'm used to trying to make myself invisible, but they're clearly not. I make a face as Hallie steps on a twig and the sharp crack sends a bird shrieking out of the nearest tree.

'Sorry,' she whispers. 'I was built for action, not stealth.'

I give her a half-smile, while Naira tuts, wait a few seconds, then carry on. Past the house, to where their back garden must be, though it's hidden behind the fence. I hear the cluck of chickens and someone – I'm guessing Mrs Latchitt – humming the same tune that Mr Latchitt was whistling as we came through the school gates. I find a knothole in the timber fence, big enough to look through. I put my eye to it while the others hover behind me, trying to look over my shoulder, even though they wouldn't be able to see anything. I'm not used to having people so far into my space, and it makes me uncomfortable.

I see Mrs Latchitt walking slowly down a winding, stepping-stone path, bent slightly against the freezing wind that has started whipping around us. She's draped in layers of clothes – a long skirt and coat with a thick shawl over the top, a woollen scarf and a knitted hat pulled low over her face. Only part of her face and her bony hands are visible. Strange that she's not wearing gloves. She hums that familiar tune that I still can't place, but in a high-pitched warble that makes my skin crawl.

'Is she trying to ward off evil spirits?' Gus whispers. 'That singing will keep the ghost away for sure.'

'Shush,' Naira whispers back. 'What's she doing, Angelo?'

'She's going to the chicken coops, I think. They have two henhouses in the garden. Maybe she's collecting eggs.'

'Terrifying,' Naira whispers, not needing to be loud for me to hear the sarcasm in her voice. 'This is pointless.'

'Spying on little old ladies is *never* pointless,' Gus whispers. 'Oh wait, that sounded wrong.'

'So wrong,' Hallie sniggers.

Mrs Latchitt creaks open the door to one of the chicken coops, straining against the wind that wants to keep it shut. She scoops up a chicken and tucks it under her arm, singing gently to it as she closes the door, lowers the latch and follows the stone path further down the yard. At the other end of the yard, there's a crumbling circular stone structure, about a metre high, and covered with a wooden lid the thickness of my arm. It looks like an old well. A large tree stump rises from the scraggly grass next to it, an axe resting blade-down in the top of the stump. Mrs Latchitt stops at the well, cooing at the chicken like it's a human baby, and stroking its rust-coloured feathers. My brain feels slow and sluggish – I can't think what she's up to. I try to calculate the possibilities as I watch her squeeze the chicken tighter under her arm, so hard that she must be hurting it, while her other hand takes hold of the lid of the well. It's huge and heavy – it must weigh fifty kilos – and I know she can't possibly lift it. But she does. She pulls it off like it's nothing, and places it carefully beside her, leaning up against the well. Underneath is a gaping black hole that she leans over and looks into, peering down like it goes deep under the ground.

She grabs the chicken with her right hand again, dangling it upside down by its feet. Still singing that wretched tune. The chicken flaps and struggles. And just as I latch on to an awful thought, the idea unfurling in my mind like a tentacled monster oozing from a cave, she raises it higher, then with an actual whoop of glee, she throws it into the well.

I almost cry out.

'What the hell was that?' Hallie tugs my arm. 'Angelo?'

'Dude,' Gus says. 'What happened?'

'Just a minute,' I hiss back, my heart thudding so hard it makes me feel sick. And though I expect an argument, they fall silent and wait while I watch.

Mrs Latchitt gazes down into the well, her face lit up, making her look like an entirely different person. 'So long, little chicken.' She giggles like a toddler, clapping her hands.

I gasp and drop to the ground, crouching with my hands on the floor to steady me, trying to understand what I've just seen.

'What is it?' Naira says. 'Would you move? I'm looking now.' And she pushes me with her foot so she can stand in front of the hole.

'Are you OK?' Hallie crouches down next to me.

'There's something weird going on,' I whisper,

noticing an absence of noise that was there a moment ago. The wind is building, rushing past my ears and making trees creak, but it's quieter than it was.

'I can't even see her,' Naira hisses.

And that's when I realise that Mrs Latchitt has stopped humming.

I stand up. 'Can I look?' I say. Naira shrugs and steps away from the hole. I put my eye to it again, seeing everything in the Latchitts' yard as it was when I last looked – the chicken coops, the tree stump, the well with its lid leaning against the side – except Mrs Latchitt has gone. I carefully push myself against the fence, my eye straining to see the furthest corners of the garden. She can't have just disappeared.

I swear out loud as my view is suddenly obscured by an eye on the opposite side of the hole, watching me back.

CHAPTER FOUR

CANNIBALS

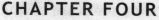

The eye blinks once, then fixes on mine again. It's washed-out grey and crisscrossed with bloodshot lines.

'Who's there?' Mrs Latchitt says. 'I see you, brown eyes. Aren't you going to say hello?'

I drop to the ground again, and the others drop too. It's instinct, I think. They don't know what's happened, but they can feel the wrongness of it.

'Come here, child. It's not me you need to be afraid of.'

I don't know what to do. Stand up, say hi and

41

act casual, or run away as fast as I can? The others are watching me, waiting to follow my lead. None of them are saying anything for once. I realise hiding isn't an option – she knows that we're here and she knows who we are. We can't get out of school without her husband unlocking the gates. I make the decision. I stand up.

'Hi, Mrs Latchitt,' I say, stepping back from the fence a little. 'Sorry to bother you – we were looking for Mr Latchitt and thought he might be in the yard.'

'He's not here now. Why do you need him?' She stares through the hole, her eye watering slightly as the wind blows stronger.

'We can't find our teacher, Mr Canton.' Naira stands next to me. 'We thought Mr Latchitt might be able to help us.'

'Come to the front gate,' Mrs Latchitt says. 'You can wait in the house. I'll make some tea.'

'Um, we're OK, thanks,' Gus says. 'We'll just look around some more. Out here.'

'I have biscuits.' The corner of her eye crinkles up like she's smiling. 'There's not a child alive who can say no to one of my biscuits.'

Gus nudges me hard in the ribs.

'We'll come round,' I say, because I want her to go away. I need to tell the others what I saw.

'I'll put some extra logs on the fire,' she says, and disappears.

We back away from the fence and stand in a huddle facing each other, far enough away that she'd not be able to hear us if she was still listening at the fence. I picture her, ear to the rough wood, witchy fingers resting in the ivy, silently watching and waiting.

'I told you,' Gus says. 'Out-of-date biscuits.'

'We have more to worry about than expired food,' I say.

'Tell us what you saw, step by step,' Hallie says. 'What was she shouting about?'

'She collected a chicken; took it over to a circular stone wall; lifted a chunk of wood the size of a truck wheel off the top if it; dangled the chicken upside down; threw it like a penny into a freaking wishing well; and *really* enjoyed it.' I rub my face hard enough to hurt a little.

'That is not what I was expecting you to say,' Gus says. 'I mean, I had put together a list of likely explanations, and wishing-welling a chicken didn't even make the top twenty.'

'But she's so old and weak,' Naira says. 'You're telling me she lifted that enormous well cover by herself?'

'I'm telling you she lifted it like it weighed nothing. She lifted it with one hand, so she could squeeze the chicken with the other. Then as she threw the chicken in, she literally whooped like it was the best time of her life.'

'That's disgusting,' Hallie says. 'What sort of person treats an innocent animal like that?'

'But why throw a chicken down a well?' Gus frowns. 'Did she want to kill it? And, more importantly, I wonder what she wished for?'

'You seem very comfortable talking about chicken murder,' Hallie says.

Gus shrugs. 'Just saying.'

'He's right,' I say. 'If she wanted to kill it, for food, or because it was sick, she could have just axed it on the stump or broken its neck. There must be a reason for throwing it down the well.'

'Maybe she's just completely unhinged,' says Naira.

I shrug because I don't know. I have a few thoughts on it, but I'd rather not say until I have more information. 'If there is a reason, I'm sure it can't be good.'

'I'm reporting her for animal cruelty,' Hallie says, literally pushing up her sleeves like she's going in for a scrap. 'Right after I've told that old witch what I think of her.' She starts marching across the grass towards the front of the Latchitts'. 'She should be arrested.'

'Stop and think, you idiot.' Naira runs after her and grabs her arm, spinning her back around to face us. 'We're stuck in these grounds with no way to call for help. Mr Canton has disappeared, this mad woman is doing weird things with chickens and trying to lure us into her house for who knows what reason, and you want to go knocking on her door.'

'You think she's Hansel and Greteling us?' Gus gasps. 'Feeding us up with cookies till we get nice and fat, then cooking us on the fire and eating us?'

'If she was eating people, I think she'd be healthier looking,' I say. 'Human flesh has high nutritional value.'

'How the hell do you know that?' Naira shouts. 'Are you all psychopaths? Am I stuck in the first detention of my life with a pack of cannibals?'

'Calm down, Naira,' Gus says. 'If I was choosing someone to eat, it definitely would not be you.'

'Are you saying I'm fat?' Hallie shouts.

'What? No. Where did that come from?' Gus throws his hands in the air.

Hallie is fuming. 'You're saying you wouldn't

eat Naira, obviously because she's skinny, which implies that you'd eat me because I'm curvier.'

'It really doesn't,' Gus says. 'I just don't think Naira would taste very nice. Too uptight.'

'How would being uptight make me taste bad?' Naira looks furious.

'People do say that happier animals make tastier meat,' I say. 'That's why rich people buy free-range, organic stuff.'

'You guys are sick,' Hallie huffs. 'So glad I'm a vegetarian.'

This is getting us nowhere. I take a breath, try to calm down. 'The point is that Mrs Latchitt is unlikely to try to eat us if we go to her house.'

'Then she'll probably just murder us and stuff our bodies so she can keep us around her house like creepy dolls,' Gus says.

'She needs to be stopped.' Hallie starts walking off. 'I'll go on my own – I can take her down by myself.'

'Should I rugby tackle her?' Gus says.

Naira runs after her and grabs her by the shoulder. 'Stop, Hallie!'

Hallie turns and shoves her hard, sending Naira stumbling backwards and on to the muddy ground. 'Look what you've done!' Naira roars, and immediately starts crying, loud, low sobs like the kind you only usually see in the movies when someone's best friend dies. It's unexpected, and I hesitate, not sure what to do.

Hallie stops and turns, looking down at Naira with something like guilt on her face. 'Why are you crying? Did I hurt you?'

Naira just sits, her face in her hands. We all crouch next to her.

'I'm sorry, Naira,' Hallie says. 'I didn't mean to push you.'

'Looked like you did,' Gus says. 'You literally turned around like a raging bull, put your bull hooves on her and shoved. I can re-enact it for you if you like.'

'I meant I didn't intend to,' Hallie says.

'I lost my temper, and I do things when I'm angry that I feel awful about. I'm sorry, Naira, are you OK?'

Naira looks up. 'I'm fine. It's just . . . this.' She indicates her PE kit covered in mud. 'I'll have to show it to my mum.'

'We're about to get murdered and you're worried about your dirty PE kit?' Gus says. 'Not trying to be funny, but I don't get your priorities.'

'I get it,' I say. Naira comes from the same estate that I do, where things don't come easily. 'But you know, it's not ripped or damaged at all. The mud will wash off. Your mum may be mad but she'll get over it. You don't have PE again until, what – Tuesday?' Naira nods. 'Enough time to get it cleaned up.'

'Don't you have a spare?' Hallie says, looking distraught. 'Here, take mine. We'll switch.' And she starts taking off her sweatshirt in the middle of the field. Me and Gus instantly cover our eyes, deeply uncomfortable about the situation we've somehow ended up in.

'Stop!' Naira says. 'We have enough going on without you running around the field in your underwear.'

'But I want to fix this,' Hallie says.

'You can't,' Naira says. 'It's done.' A silent moment passes. 'But I appreciate the thought.'

I reach out a hand to Naira, expecting her not to take it. But she does, and I pull her up.

'Thanks, Angelo.' She smiles, her cheeks still glistening with tears and snot. Gus pulls a ragged tissue from somewhere and hands it to her.

'From now on we stick together,' I say. 'Agreed?'

Everyone nods, and I feel a shift. The wind around us is howling, as the weather gets wilder by the minute, but between us something has eased.

'Let's knock at the Latchitts', tell her we appreciate the offer but we're going to keep searching for Mr Canton and Arabella,' I say. 'We'll be polite, but flat refuse to go in. There are four of us and one of her – she can't force us inside, even if she does have supernatural strength.'

We walk towards the Latchitts' front gate.

'Out of interest,' Gus says, 'what do you think I would taste like?'

'Spicy fajitas with guac and sour cream,' Naira says, like she's been thinking about it for a while.

'I was gonna say risotto,' Hallie says. 'But not a smooth one – the kind with loads of lumps of weird mushrooms that look like they've been dug up in an enchanted forest.'

'Hawaiian pizza with a stuffed crust full of strong cheese, and barbecue dip on the side,' I add.

'Aw, thanks, guys,' Gus sniffs. 'Those are the nicest things anyone's ever said to me.'

And for the first time in what already feels like a long day, we all laugh.

CHAPTER FIVE

PEP TALK

I knock on the front door and step back, watching as a flake of white paint comes away from the wood and disappears into the wind. The hanging baskets either side of the entrance are rattling their chains, the flowers in them withered, their blackened leaves curled like dead spiders.

The door opens and Mrs Latchitt appears, her face grey and unreadable. 'I was afraid you'd had a terrible accident,' she says. 'You took so long.'

'I slipped over on the field,' Naira says.

'Slipped, did you?' Mrs Latchitt eyeballs Naira's muddy clothes.

'That's right.' Naira does the smile she saves for teachers when she wants extra merit points.

'Well, come in then, and I'll put that uniform in the washer and make you some tea. I have something you can wear while you're waiting.'

Gus makes a squeaking sound that I try to ignore.

'Thanks, but we can't come in,' I say. 'Mr Canton told us to search for the missing pig, so we're going to keep at it until he comes back.'

'We're here for a consequence,' Hallie adds. 'It would be wrong to take a break without permission. And we're very worried about Arabella anyway, so . . .'

'Missing pig, you say?' Mrs Latchitt blinks at us. 'I wonder what fate befell it.'

'Probably befell down a well,' Gus whispers, and Naira coughs to cover it.

'Hopefully she's just wandered into a store cupboard looking for food,' I say, thinking about that scrap of white material we found in the grass, and wondering if it's connected to Mrs Latchitt and her well. 'We'll check out the school building.'

'If you're sure.' Mrs Latchitt blinks again. 'Then I'll not hold you here against your will.'

'Thanks for your kind offer, Mrs Latchitt,' Naira says. 'But we feel this is the right thing to do.'

We turn and walk up the garden path, closing the gate behind us without looking back. I know she'll be watching. We head towards the pig yard in case Mr Canton has turned up there looking for us.

'I wonder what clothes she was going to put you in?' Hallie pulls a pack of gum out of her pocket and offers it round.

Gus snorts. 'She meant she was going to give Naira the skin of one of her previous victims. That was obvious.'

'Or something made of chicken feathers,' I add. 'Imagine if we'd gone in and she brought out a tray of bacon sandwiches.' And it shouldn't be funny, but it is. So we laugh again, because it's such a weird day, and we really have no idea what we're going to do about any of it.

We're twenty metres or so from the pig yard when Mr Canton stumbles out of the storage room. It's so unexpected that it takes a couple of seconds for it to sink in, and in that time he spots us too.

'Kids,' he shouts. 'Thank god.' He tries to run towards us, but something's not right. He's unsteady and uncoordinated, and as we get closer I see that he's bleeding from a gash on the side of his head. The blood is running down over his ear, which drips with red, soaking his tracksuit top.

We run over to him as he puts a hand against the stone wall of the building to stop himself from falling.

'Jesus, sir, are you OK?' Hallie says.

'I'm fine, thank you,' he says. 'And please

mind your language, Hallie – remember we're in school.'

Naira runs into the storage room, rushing out with a wad of paper towels. I press them against the cut on Mr Canton's head. 'What happened?' I ask.

'Now I don't want you to panic,' Mr Canton says. 'There's no reason to be alarmed and it's important that we all stay calm.' He pauses, like he's figuring out what to say.

'Just tell us,' Hallie says. 'We're not kids.'

'Did Arabella do this to you, sir?' Gus says. 'Has she gone rogue?'

'No, Arabella is not responsible for my injury,' he says. 'Has there been any sign of her, by the way?'

'Nothing,' Naira says. 'And stop stalling. We can handle whatever it is you have to tell us.'

He sighs, takes another wad of tissue and presses it to his cut, wincing a little, then smiling to try to hide it. 'Right,' he says. 'I'll level with you. I was in the mansion looking for Mr Latchitt when something hit me. It came from behind, so I didn't see what it was. I fell unconscious and everything in my brain is rather muddled, I'm afraid, because when I came around, I couldn't remember how I'd got where I was.'

'What do you mean?' I say.

'I mean, I woke up somewhere else from the place I remember being hit. I must have wandered around when I was semi-conscious.'

'And when you say something hit you,' Gus says, 'how are you thinking that happened? Like an inanimate object came alive and flung itself at you?'

'Well, that's another thing I'm not sure about,' Mr Canton says.

I can see what he's not wanting to say. 'Is it possible someone attacked you?' I ask. 'Like the others said, we can handle the truth, and we'd rather know than not.'

Mr Canton's bloody face lights up with a huge grin. 'I am loving this use of "we", all of a sudden. Is it possible that you guys have started working as a hashtag "Back On Track" team?'

We all groan.

'Proud of you,' Mr Canton says. 'Whatever's happened today has been worth it.'

'This isn't a set-up, is it?' Gus asks. 'You faked the missing pig and your . . .' he does the inverted commas gesture with his fingers, 'accident, so that we'd have to talk to each other. Like some messed-up escape room.'

Mr Canton chuckles. 'I love the way your mind works, Gustav. And though I can't take credit for that this time around, it's definitely worth thinking about for the future.'

'Can we please focus on the fact that there might be a violent criminal in the school grounds?' Naira says.

'And a pig abductor,' says Hallie.

'Quite right, yes, let's do that.' Mr Canton takes the tissues from his head and puts his hand up to check the cut. 'I think that's stopped bleeding now, so let's make our way to student services to get some hot drinks and regroup. I think, given the circumstances, I'd better call your parents and record the morning's unexpected events.'

He sets off at a jog, looking back over his shoulder to call, 'Come on, knees high, let's get you warmed up.'

'I'm good with getting a hot chocolate, but there's no way I'm running,' Hallie says. 'I feel like I've done enough exercise for one day.'

'Same,' Gus says, and we all start to walk.

Mr C is about ten metres ahead of us, doing some kind of power jog that involves a lot of elbow and knee movement. The guy's just been smashed over the head and he's still trying to set a good example.

'That looks exhausting,' I say.

'Totally.' Naira's retying her ponytail.

'The man's a machine,' Gus says.

Mr Canton turns towards us, still jogging, but backwards and more slowly. 'What we need

here, guys, is a positive mental attitude.'
He keeps jogging backwards. 'Has it been a
rough morning so far? Yes. Has it thrown up
unexpected challenges? Undoubtedly. But think
about how you've dealt with it. Like superstars.
If that's not a reason to feel optimistic, I don't
know what is.'

'You should probably look where you're
going,' Hallie shouts back, as he almost trips
on an uneven patch of ground.

'I don't need to look,' he calls back. 'Because
I have faith in myself to make it safely across this
field. We have the power to decide our fates,
and they do say that I put the can in "Can –"'

And then he's gone. In less than a second, he
disappears into the ground. It happens so fast
that I can hardly take it in. I'm aware
of screams beside me – Gus and Naira,
I think, and I must stop dead in my tracks,
because suddenly I find myself starting to
move. I sprint towards the place where Mr
Canton was standing a moment before but

which is now just a patch of field.

I'm maybe five metres away when it's like the ground opens up in front of me. Mr Canton's face rises out of the earth, his arms reaching towards me, grasping at clumps of grass that just tear away in his hands. He's scrabbling with blackened fingertips, trying to hold on, to pull himself out. And I'm so close. I lunge forward, trying to grab his hand, seeing nothing but the terrified look on his paper-white face – smears of blood, eyes wide, mouth open in shock.

As I skid across the ground on my stomach, stretching so hard I feel my muscles strain to the point of snapping, he makes a desperate surge forward. My hands are centimetres from his, separated by nothing but a slice of freezing November air. His eyes fix on mine. 'Get inside,' he says. 'Call for help.' And then just as the tips of my fingers make contact with his battered ones, he jerks back. Like he's been yanked from below. Like he's in the jaws of some invisible monster. My eyes flick to the darkness underneath him, and I swear I see something moving down there: an arm, or a leg, dark and slim, darting further up Mr Canton's body to get a better grip. I clutch at Mr C with everything I have, but my hands slip. The last thing I see is the horror on his face. Fear like I've never witnessed before.

I lie still for a moment, hands clutching at air, staring at the place in front of me where a second before there was a gaping hole and my teacher's horrified face. Now there's nothing. The ground has sealed up. Mr Canton is gone.

CHAPTER SIX

TREMORS

'Angelo?'

I realise Hallie has her hand on my shoulder, shaking me. I'm face down on the grass, lungs burning, heart pounding, my ears filled with the sound of either my own blood crashing around my body, or the raging wind, I'm not sure which.

Bit by bit, the world becomes clear again.

Gus is bent over, vomiting into the grass, while Naira paces up and down next to him, stopping every now and then to put a hand gently on his back.

And Hallie is talking to me. I look up to see her lips moving, and her face the colour of two-day-old tea.

'Angelo? Are you OK?'

I push myself off the ground until I'm kneeling, eyes scanning the area in front of me. 'I'm fine,' I say. 'I'm fine. We need to dig. We need to get him out.' I'm not fine. The thought of being sucked under the ground and dying in the dark under piles of earth horrifies me. I can't think of a worse way to go.

I start clawing at the earth in front of me, trying to find a weakness. Hallie kneels down and does the same, fingernails prising at rock-hard turf, achieving nothing.

'How can there be a hole here one second, and nothing the next?' she says.

Two other pairs of hands join ours and we all scrabble pointlessly. Nothing loosens. Nothing shifts. 'Not possible,' I say, roaring in frustration. I stand and start kicking at the ground, raging and cursing in a way that Mr

Canton would definitely not approve of. I wonder if he can hear me. The others back off as I do exactly nothing to the surface of the field but do manage to hurt my toes a lot. Eventually, when I'm sweating and gasping for breath, and the patch of ground is still staring up at me like I'm not even an annoyance, I stop.

'You OK, bud?' Gus takes a step towards me. 'Well, not OK, but you know what I mean.'

I nod.

'What the hell was that?' Hallie says. 'What just happened?'

'Did he fall?' Naira looks at me. Her eyes are full of something I've not seen since Year 2 when she slipped on a wet drain cover and grazed half the skin off her knee. 'He fell, right? There was a hole in the ground, like a sinkhole, and he fell.'

'There was a hole,' I say. 'But if it was a sinkhole, we'd be able to see it.'

'So maybe the ground is shifting and it refilled, like a small earthquake.' Gus spits into the grass next to him. 'Sorry, just getting rid of the last chunks.'

'There was no warning, though,' says Hallie. 'No rumbling, no shaking. And it was just in that one exact spot.'

'I should have saved him,' I say. 'I was so close. If I'd been faster, or stronger . . .'

'And if I'd have spent more time doing cardio instead of watching anime for the past year, I could have saved him,' Gus says. 'It's not your fault.'

'He's right,' Naira says. 'I'm fast. I could have reached him, but I froze. At least you tried. If it's anyone's fault it's mine.'

'It's nobody's fault,' Hallie shouts. 'It was an accident. A freak, unpredictable accident.'

We look at the place where Mr Canton once stood.

'I don't know if it was,' I say.

'What?' Naira looks at me.

'I don't know if it was an accident. I don't think he fell.'

'You're in shock, mate,' Gus says. 'You're imagining things that weren't there. He fell. We all saw him.'

I shake my head. 'Nah, it doesn't fit. He had a chance to pull himself back up. He tried, but something was stopping him.'

'Something like what?' Hallie asks.

'I don't know,' I say. 'He was climbing out, then he was yanked back down, like something had hold of him. He was fighting more than just the earth, Hal. There's something down there, under the ground.'

They all stare at me. Trying to make up their minds about how mental I am. I can understand why they'd want to believe it was an accident; that he fell. But I know in my bones that there was more to it.

I feel suddenly weak and tired, like my legs aren't mine any more and I don't know how to stand up. I slump on to the grass, noticing but not caring about how cold it is. I pull my knees up, wrap my arms around them and tuck my head down, burying my chin into my chest. I feel someone sit next to me, and an arm around my shoulder. Hallie. Then someone sits on my other side, leaning up against me, creating a warm patch down my left side. Naira.

'Can I be part of this Angelo sandwich?' Gus says, sitting cross-legged in front of me and sweeping his arms around all of us.

'Aw, Gus, you're the bread,' Hallie's muffled voice says.

'We don't ever speak of this again,' says Naira, and I find myself smiling even with all the hell that has just gone down.

When we lean back out of the hug, my heart is calmer and my head less heavy.

'We should try to get into the school building and call the police,' I say. 'Come on.'

'Hold up,' Gus says as I start to stand. 'What's that on your shoe?'

I look down at my trainers – once white but now scuffed with grass stains and dirt. There's a shred of something stuck to the toe of one of them – it's practically transparent, but when I pull it off and hold it up to my eyes, I see what it is.

'It's the same stuff we found in the pig yard.'

Gus takes the other end between his fingers and pulls it. It stretches out, finer and clearer until it's like a thread connecting us. I expect it to snap, but it doesn't. A drop of the rain that's been threatening all day falls from the darkening sky and lands on the thread, balancing there in a crystal-like globule, bouncing up and down in the wind.

All morning I've felt like my brain is failing to put things together properly: stuff I should be able to remember – information that I know is in there somewhere – circling around me just out of reach. But as I look at that strand, it's like it connects some of the random thoughts in my head. I spend a lot of the time stuck at home, just me and my brother in a small, messy flat. At night I stay up late watching TV – shows about science and nature.

They give me a chance to see what's out there in the world. All those hours of documentaries mean I know a lot about wildlife – plants, animals, insects. The dread I'm feeling now is because the path my thoughts are heading down leads somewhere impossible.

'I know what this stuff looks like,' I say, staring at it, horror bubbling up inside me. 'And if it is what I think, we need to get off the grass. Now.'

'But . . .' Naira starts.

'Later,' I say, already two steps ahead. 'Run now, talk later.' I break into a sprint, heading for the closest way off the field. The others start jogging behind me with an infuriating lack of urgency. 'If you don't want to end up like Mr Canton,' I shout, the rain starting to lash down, 'you're going to need to run faster.'

Thunder booms above us, less like a crash and more like a motorway pile-up, and it gives them the jolt they need to shift. Naira's fast, and crazy competitive, and she soon powers past me towards the tennis courts. I turn to see Hallie and Gus, behind me but not too far, running flat out. The rain is coming down so heavily that it's hard to see clearly, but I swear I notice a movement in the ground close to their feet.

'Go!' I shout, as loudly as I can. I don't know if they can hear me above the storm, but they must see the panic in my eyes because they find enough juice to push harder, their legs pumping, grimaces on their faces. *Don't fall*, I think. *Don't fall, don't fall, don't fall.*

I keep up the pace until I reach Naira on the paved area between the mansion and the main block. Hallie and Gus race up seconds later and the four of us spend the next minute coughing our guts up, bent double, not giving a crack about the rain or the wind, just relieved to be on solid ground.

'You want to tell us what's going on?' Hallie says. 'Because I hope I didn't just kill myself running unless there was a good reason.'

I go to flick my hair out of my face before remembering that it's basically being hammered on to my face by an ocean of rain. 'OK,' I say, slicking it back with my hands. 'This is going to sound crazy, but it also fits. Sort of.'

'Before we listen to your mad theories, we need to find a phone,' Naira says. 'Our teacher just fell down a hole, for flip's sake. Let's get inside, out of this awful rain, and call for help.' She starts walking off before I can argue.

'If only we had our phones,' Hallie says, the look of longing on her face cut short, probably by the memory of what happened to the guy who had our phones zipped up in his bumbag.

'RIP, phones,' Gus says. 'Thank you for your service.' He doesn't look too great. I mean, none of us look great, but he looks like he's struggling the most.

'You OK, man?' I say.

'Yeah, living my best life right now,' he grins, but there's something in his face that makes me think he's fronting.

'What's wrong? You look like you're dying,' Hallie stands in front of him, putting the back of her hand on his forehead and trying to force him to make eye contact with her by shoving hers about three centimetres from his. 'Are you ill?'

'I'm peachy.' Gus tries to dodge past her, but she's relentless. 'Apart from being cold and wet, having a mouth that tastes of puke, and an annoying girl in my face.'

'We should go after Naira,' I say. 'She's right that we need to get inside and find a phone. Then I need to check something out.'

The closest building is the main block, where we stood in student services just an hour ago. Was it even an hour? I have no way of knowing the time, lost without my phone. Feels longer. In student services there are phones, warmth and vending machines, and honestly there's nothing I want more at the moment. But Naira is already pulling at the front door, and it's locked.

'Why would they lock it when we're all still here?' Naira says, turning to us.

We run up the paved concourse to the music and art blocks, trying doors and windows with no joy.

'The mansion was open when we went looking for Mr Canton earlier,' Gus says. 'Let's try there.'

But the mansion is locked too. We stand on the drive, the rain easing now to a light patter, pushed around by the wind.

'You think Mr Latchitt's locked everything on purpose?' Hallie says. 'So that we have to go to his gingerbread house?'

'I think maybe he has,' I say. 'I don't know for sure how Mr and Mrs Latchitt have anything to do with what happened to Mr Canton, but there's been enough weird stuff going on to make me want to stay well clear of them.'

'So we're stuck outside in this infuriating weather,' Naira shouts and stomps her foot down into the gravel, sending tiny chips of stone flying. 'A consequence should not involve making pupils sick with hypothermia.'

'Total breach of our human rights,' Hallie says. 'I'll be organising a protest as soon as we're out of here.' Hallie is always protesting about something. We've only been here a few months and I've already seen her fight against the sexist uniform policy, the lack of diversity in the teaching staff, and the school's fascist approach to hairstyles. I used to think it was annoying that everything offended her, but now I see it's just her way of trying to make the world a better place.

'I think I have a banner at home you can use for that,' Gus says. 'NO TO DEATHTENTIONS.'

'Deathtentions is a good idea for a movie, actually,' I say.

'Can we focus?' Naira asks. 'What's our next move?'

I toe the gravel with my trainer, trying to calculate which course of action is the least likely to end in trouble. The drive is uneven, with ridges like the crests of stony waves, and dips where rainwater has collected in puddles that lie still and flat. I realise the storm has stopped as suddenly as it started, which is something at least. But as I stare at the ground beneath me I see a shudder move across the puddles. They wobble, then settle back into stillness. A couple of pieces of gravel slip down one of the ridges, clicking against each other as they rest at the edge of a dip. It feels like my heart stops.

'Have you guys seen *Jurassic Park*?' I say, watching the surface water with held breath.

'And how is that helpful right now?' Naira asks. 'We have more important things to worry about.'

'Look at the puddles,' I say.

'Are you serious?' Hallie says. 'What are you on about?'

'Just look at them.' I raise my voice a bit. It's enough to make them shut up and pay attention.

A sharp-angled pebble shifts in the space between our feet, and a puddle ripples, goes still for a few seconds, then ripples again. More stones slide, slipping down peaks and into the flat water below.

'Is something . . . moving down there?' Naira asks.

'What the hell is it?' Hallie says.

The gravel moves again, more pronounced this time, and I feel something give way under my foot.

'We're not safe here,' I say. 'On three we run around to the new quad, then across the paved area to the science block. OK?'

None of them speak, they just stare at the ground in horror.

'Guys?' I say. 'On three, follow me. OK?'

'OK,' Naira says.

'Yeah.' Hallie doesn't raise her eyes.

'Is this the electric fence bit?' Gus says. 'Because I don't want to be the kid that gets electrocuted.'

'No fence,' I say. 'But we have to get off the ground.'

'On three,' Gus says. 'Or after three? Like one, two, three, go?'

'On three.'

'Got it.'

'One.' I take a breath as another movement below us sends a trickle of gravel chips skittering into a puddle. 'Two.' The water ripples again – harder this time then flattens out. 'Three!'

And I spring forward, lifting my knees high, trying to have as little contact with the ground as possible. Every time my foot hits the drive I expect to fall, or worse. The others are just a second behind me. We're crunching heavily in the gravel, but there's no other way of getting through – we have to hope that our speed is enough.

A roar of sound behind me makes me turn to see stones waterfalling down as a hole opens up in the place we were standing just a moment earlier. The others turn too, mouths hanging open, shock and curiosity overcoming their fear, just for a second. I want to see what's there – what's making the ground swallow the gravel – but more than that I want to survive.

'Go!' I shout. So we run. We run like the floor is caving in around us, like a river of lava is rolling towards us, like we're being chased by a freaking tyrannosaurus rex. We don't look back again.

CHAPTER SEVEN

TIME TO BREATHE

I grab the handle of the science-block door, expecting it to be locked like all the others, but it swings open, offering us an escape from the outside. We're plunged into total darkness as the door bangs shut behind us.

'Why the hell aren't the lights coming on?' Hallie swears.

'This is an old building – the lights are manual,' I say, trying to remember if I've ever noticed a control panel. 'Feel around, the switch must be close.'

'Got it,' Gus says, and the lights flick on, one at a time, slowly filling the hallway with light. We're just inside the entrance area, looking into a large, multi-sided space with doors leading off into the different labs and offices. Everything here is irregular – each lab a random shape and size, and the offices sit in odd corners, jutting out into the hall. It seems to be deserted. There's no sight or sound of anybody. The floor is concrete covered in grey rubber tiles. It's solid.

We check all the office doors, hoping to find a working phone. But they're all locked. The classrooms are open though, so cold, empty and echoey that they look like different rooms to the ones we spend time in during school. We go into the biology one. The stools are set messily on the benches, thrown up there yesterday by the last class, desperate to get out of school and enjoy the weekend. I can almost hear the scraping and banging as everyone raced out. Without saying a word, it's like we all agree that this is where we stop. We don't bother with the stools, just sink to the ground, propped against walls, trying to breathe. Trying to think. It crosses my mind that it was a little too convenient that the science-block door was open when the rest of the school is locked up. But we needed to rest, and there was nowhere else to go.

There's nothing we can do about our soaking clothes, but at least we're out of the wind, and man it feels good to sit.

'I have biology in here on Thursdays,' Gus says, looking around the room. 'Look, you see that ink spatter on the wall right there?' He points at a spray of dark blue that stands out against the chipped yellow paint. 'I did that on the first week to annoy the girl sitting next to me.'

'I hate seating plans,' Hallie says. 'Like we're too immature to choose where we should be.'

'Yeah, me too,' Gus says.

'I bet the girl who sits next to you hates them too,' Naira says. 'I mean, what was the point of flicking ink at her?'

'It seemed funny at the time,' Gus says. He frowns then, and turns to look across the other side of the room. 'It was probably the least awful thing I did to her. She doesn't sit next to me any more. That's part of the reason why I'm here.'

'What do you mean?' Hallie asks. 'I thought you were here because of the dining-hall riot, the same as the rest of us.'

'It's complicated,' Gus says, and stares down at the floor.

'So,' Naira breaks the silence that follows first. 'As we're all no doubt thinking the same thing, we'd better get to the point. I have questions.'

'Does anyone else need the toilet?' Gus says. I don't know if he really needs the toilet or if it's an excuse to escape in case the questions are about what he just told us.

'Not what I was thinking,' Naira sighs. 'But yeah.'

'There are staff toilets just past chemistry two on the right,' Hallie says.

'Staff toilets?' Gus jumps up. 'Now you're talking.' He jogs off down the hall, and we hear him open the door and whoop. 'Jasmine hand cream? What is this life?'

We all laugh as he closes the door behind him.

'Is he all right, do you think?' Hallie asks. 'You know he has loads of authorised absences on Thursday mornings. I heard he has some medical thing.'

'I never heard that,' I say.

'You don't hear anything, Angelo, because you walk around all silent and depressed the entire time.' Naira rolls her eyes.

'I do not,' I say, surprised that anyone has noticed anything about me when I try so hard to stay under the radar.

'Yeah, you do,' Hallie says. 'You have that whole lone-wolf thing going on.' She puts on a voice and flips imaginary hair out of her eyes. 'Oh, hey, I'm Angelo, and I'm so deep and moody. Don't even look at me.'

'Wait, was that supposed to be me?' I say. 'Because you sounded nothing like me.'

'I thought it was quite good, actually,' Naira says.

'Shall I do you next?' Hallie asks.

'No!' Naira shouts, at the same time that I say, 'Yes.'

'Oh wait,' Hallie says, looking around on the floor. 'I just have to find a stick to put up my butt first.'

Gus comes back to find us all laughing. 'What have I missed?'

'Naira's butt stick,' I say.

'Unfair!' Gus says. 'Pull it out and let me meet it formally – I'd like to shake its hand for doing such an outstanding job.'

Naira's cheeks go pink. 'Shall we get back to

talking about the life-or-death situation we're currently in the middle of?'

'Ugh.' Gus rolls his eyes. 'Boring.'

'Yeah, I guess we should,' I say.

'You know something, Angelo,' Naira says. 'Or you've guessed something. We need to know.'

'OK,' I say. 'Follow me.'

'Great,' Hallie says. 'After I've used the toilet. I want to try that hand cream.'

'It's luxurious,' Gus says. 'Feel my hand. Feel it.'

'Ooh, that's so soft!' Hallie squeaks. 'Feel Gus's hand, Naira.'

'But the situation . . .'

'Didn't you need to go too, though?' Hallie says.

'Well, yes, but I can probably hold it.'

'You should never hold it, Naira, it does terrible things to your body. My auntie's dog walker's hairdresser held her pee in too often and she ended up in a coma.'

'She did not.' Naira frowns. 'But I'll go if you promise not to tell me all about it.'

In the end we all go, including Gus for a second time. When it's my turn, I realise that it's the first time I've been alone since I got to school. Normally I go out of my way to be away from people – I'm not bothered about having friends because they just make life more complicated. But as I hear the others laughing outside the toilet door, I find myself rushing so I can get back out there and be a part of it. I want to be around them, I realise. It's a strange and unexpected FOMO that I'm half worried I'm going to regret later. Then we're finally ready to go and walking to the far corner of the block where I'm hoping we'll find some answers.

'So we're going to the animal house?' Hallie says.

'Yeah.' I nod. 'I have a theory. I need more information.'

'Am I the only person here who didn't know

the animal house existed until this moment?' Naira says, looking like she'd be happier not knowing about it.

'Nah, it's news to me too,' says Gus. 'I mean, I knew about the pigs. Everyone knows about the pigs. The pigs are the MVPs.'

Hallie pulls open the door to biology three. 'We come here sometimes for animal welfare club when we're not doing stuff with the pigs.'

'And what animals are we going to be seeing, exactly?' Naira says. 'I have a feeling they're going to be the not-cute kind.'

'There are small mammals – mice, hamsters, guinea pigs, that sort of thing,' I say. 'And some reptiles and insects – species from all over the world. They're cool.'

'And cute in their own way,' Hallie adds.

'You sound like my mum does when she's talking about me and my sister,' Gus snorts. '"Tabby is so funny and sweet and she lights up our lives every single day."' He's saying this in a fake, high-pitched, smiley voice. '"Oh yeah, and Gus is there too. He's all right, I suppose."'

We turn the handle of a door at the back of the classroom that you probably wouldn't really notice unless you knew it was there. It looks like a store cupboard.

'My parents are like that too,' Hallie says. 'They talk to my brother like he's a puppy . . . "Did you draw this picture, Curtis? No, you didn't, I can't believe it – it must have been a professional artist. Hallie, look at Curtis's picture. Look at it. Isn't it the best picture you ever saw in your entire life?"' She's feeling inside the door for the light switch. 'And with me they're like, "Hallie, you really need to think about your attitude."'

'But if you didn't have an attitude, you wouldn't be here now,' I say. 'And I'm kind of glad you are. Not because I want you to be soaking wet, freezing cold, and running for your life and stuff. But it's good to have you with us.'

I can't see Hallie's face because she's still

looking for the light switch, and it's dark as hell, but the fact that she doesn't shout at me makes me think she knows what I mean.

'Club Loser for the win,' Gus whoops. 'We can't have those smug pigs taking all the glory.'

'What about you, Angelo?' Naira asks. 'You have a little brother – is he your parents' favourite?'

'To be honest, I don't think they have a favourite . . .' I hear the flick of a switch, and I squint as the lights flicker on. 'My parents work as much as they can, so my brother and me are like our own separate team.' I smile. 'He's awesome, actually. Really smart and funny.'

We're in the storage area that leads to the animal house. It's full of newspaper, bedding and food, stacked tidily away on shelves.

'Do you have brothers and sisters, Naira?' Hallie asks.

'I'm an only child.' Naira gives us her best princess smile.

Gus snorts. 'Of course you are.'

'My mama spends all of her time trying to support me to do well and be the best that I can be . . .' She pauses.

'So you hate disappointing her,' I say.

She nods.

'And it's all on you, all of the time?' Hallie asks. 'That's tough.'

'Mama's relying on me to make a more comfortable life for myself than she's had. She has a detailed plan.'

And I think it hits us all at the same time that Naira is the way she is for a reason.

'I hear alarming squeaks coming from behind that door.' She breaks the short silence. 'I am not going to enjoy this.'

I open the door to the animal house. It's an area attached to one side of the science block, made up of four sections. Because Dread Wood High has pigs and chickens, they put a lot of focus on caring for animals, and bringing them into our learning as we go through school.

The animal house is also somewhere for kids to go if they find animals easier to be around than people. Kids like me, I guess.

The first room houses the small mammals. There are a few cages of hamsters and mice, snuffling around in sawdust, moving shredded paper in and out of tiny replica houses or stuffing their cheeks with food. We leave them to it and move into a wider space lined with water tanks. There are axolotls, their wide mouths smiling as we pass; and various types of fish, some of them flitting around in large schools, and others alone and staring silently out through the glass.

'Oh look, it's an Angelo fish,' Hallie giggles, pointing at an especially sad-looking, wide-mouthed goby.

'Oh my god, it really is,' Naira laughs.

'Shut up,' I say, but I'm smiling because even I can see the resemblance. I'm aware that my face is set to 'not interested' on good days, and 'scarily hostile' on bad ones. I don't find many things to smile about at school.

'Who ever would have thought that a fish could look so much like a human?' says Gus. 'I mean, it's incredible.'

We leave my fish twin and head to the next area, which is behind another door and dark as night because the only window is covered in a blackout blind. It's quieter than the other rooms, but that just makes the sudden rustles and chirrups that break the silence seem deceptively loud. There's a smell in here too: earthy and moist, and slightly sweet. It always makes me feel like I'm walking into an abandoned shack in the rainforest. Not that I've ever been to the rainforest, but I've watched so many documentaries that I've imagined it a thousand times. The light switch is outside the door, so I click it on before we walk in.

'What hell is this?' Naira shudders, looking around in horror.

'Insects and reptiles mostly,' I say. 'And

spiders.' I scan the tanks, checking the labels as I go, until I find what I'm looking for. 'Over here,' I call, and the others join me, staring through the glass at a habitat filled deeply with dirt that has rocks and wood chips scattered over its surface.

Naira frowns. 'Why are we looking in a spider tank?'

'That substance we found, by the pigs and on my shoe,' I say. 'I think it's spider silk.'

'Like web stuff?' Gus asks.

Everything in the tank is silent and still.

'Yeah, like web stuff. But not all spiders spin webs – some of them use it for other things.'

'I can't see a spider,' Gus says, peering into all the corners. 'Is it camouflaged?'

'No,' I say. 'It's hiding.' I open a cupboard door above the bench the tank is sitting on, and pull out a box of live crickets.

'I hope you're not going to do what I think you're going to do.' Naira takes a step back.

'I need to show you,' I say, opening the box

and gently picking out a cricket, holding it between my finger and thumb while Hallie closes the box.

I slide open the ceiling of the tank and drop the cricket on to the uneven earth. 'Now watch.' I slide the lid back and we all lean around the tank as the cricket hops about, taking in its new surroundings. It stops a while, its antennae quivering, then inches forward a few steps. I see the smallest movement in the dirt just to the right of it. My eyes flick to the others to see they're focusing on that cricket, gradually leaning in closer and closer. And then it happens. A circular lid of dirt that a moment before had been so perfectly blended into its environment that we didn't even see it, lifts up like a drain cover and a bunch of hairy legs shoot out and grab the cricket. There's less than a second of struggle, and then both the cricket and the legs are gone, the lid pulled back into the hole in the dirt. The others all jump back from the tank.

'What the hell?' Gus says.

'Trapdoor spider,' I say, grabbing a book from the shelf above the tank and flicking through to the correct page.

'But I thought spiders lived on webs,' Naira gasps. 'In the corners of ceilings and on tree branches.'

'Not all spiders,' I say. 'There are lots of spider species that are ground-dwelling.'

'And they hide in tunnels?' Gus asks.

'Some dig tunnels,' I say. 'Trapdoor spiders burrow into the ground and live there. They make their front doors out of bits of plant and earth and stick it together with their silk. Some spiders line their tunnels with the silk too.'

'You are freaking kidding me,' Gus says. 'Who knew?'

'Apparently David Attenborough over here,' says Naira, looking at me with either disgust or respect – I can't really tell which, and decide it's better not to ask.

'I hear you,' Hallie says. 'But the spider that

lives in that tank could never take down a piglet, or Mr Canton.'

'No,' I agree. 'It couldn't.'

'Do you think there's a load of them swarming down there? Like thousands of them building a mega-burrow?' Gus asks.

'That's the thing,' I say. 'Spiders are solitary. They live alone and they hunt alone.'

'Don't the females eat the males after they've mated?' Hallie says, with a grin.

'Quite often,' I say. 'And the spiderlings leave home young and never come back.'

'OK, hold up,' Naira says, staring at the spot where the cricket used to be. 'So is it possible or not?'

'Maybe. Maybe it's a new species that doesn't follow the usual spider instincts and can work as a pack.'

'It just sounds insane,' Naira says. 'There must be another, less ridiculous, option.'

I think about that flash of something I saw when I was trying to stop Mr Canton from being dragged underground. An arm or leg, I thought at the time. Too fast to be human, and the wrong shape too. I take a deep breath. If the Spiders Assemble idea seems nuts, this other possibility is going to blow their minds.

'What, Angelo?' Hallie asks. 'Just say it.'

'I have a feeling that it's one,' I say, watching the others' faces. 'A really freaking big one.'

CHAPTER EIGHT

THE WHISTLER

'I hate spiders.' Naira is going into full-on stress mode, untying and retying her ponytail so hard it looks like she's going to rip her scalp off. 'And I refuse to believe that there's one big enough to attack a teacher.'

'I saw a leg,' I say. 'When Mr Canton was going under.'

'Why didn't you tell us that?' Hallie asks.

It's a good question. 'I don't know, exactly,' I say. 'Partly because I'm used to keeping my thoughts to myself – I've never been much of a team player, as Mr Canton pointed out earlier. And I was shocked, and mad that I didn't save him, and then I doubted myself.'

'Exactly,' Naira says. 'You were shocked. You might have imagined it.'

'Or maybe it was a person dressed as a spider,' Gus says. 'Some people have really weird hobbies.'

'Why did it have to be spiders?' Naira does her ponytail AGAIN. 'I hate them.'

'Spiders are great,' I say. 'They're a vital part in the world's ecosystem. Without them we'd be overrun by bugs.'

'I hate bugs too,' she squeaks.

'Well, there you go then,' I say. 'Spiders are good guys, and for the most part they're harmless to humans.'

'Tell that to Mr Canton.' Gus makes a face. 'Oh wait, if what you say is true, you can't because he's probably being munched up right now by a man-sized spider beast.'

'It wouldn't have to be man-sized to take down a human,' I say. 'Spiders are strong. They can overcome prey much bigger than themselves.'

'So how big are we talking?' asks Hallie. 'I saw a thing on TV once that showed spiders in the rainforest that are the size of dinner plates.' She holds her hands up to demonstrate the size, although Hallie being Hallie, she adds on a good thirty centimetres extra.

'You're kidding me,' Naira says.

'But I don't think even one of those could have grabbed Mr Canton like that.'

'I've been thinking about that,' I say. 'And I'm wondering whether something might have escaped from here and found a home underground. With the right conditions, insects can get big. They used to be bigger, actually, millions of years ago.'

'What conditions?' Hallie asks.

'Not being constricted to a small enclosure,' I say. 'Being free from predators, having the right food, and preferably an oxygen-rich environment. I watched a show about this exact thing a couple of months back. There was a prehistoric dragonfly that had a wingspan of almost a metre.'

'Right, the enclosure and predator thing is possible,' Naira shudders. 'But what about the food and oxygen?'

'OK, so . . .' I grit my teeth. 'For that it would need help.'

'The Latchitts,' Hallie gasps. 'Oh my god, the chicken. Was she feeding it?'

I shrug. 'There's one way we can find out, but you're not going to like it . . .'

They look at me like I expected them to. Like I just suggested they jump out of a plane without a parachute.

'And you know, the animals in here do change quite a lot. I've come in a few times and found one of my favourites has gone – there was an awesome tarantula that I called Ellie. Still miss her.'

'Just a sec, we can check,' Hallie says. She

rushes to a cupboard by the door and starts rummaging through it, then pulls out a large, hard-backed notebook. 'It's the log of the animals here,' she says. 'It has a record of whenever they get a new one, or when something dies.' She opens it and flicks through the pages. 'Look,' she points. 'Twelve years ago a trapdoor spider died, apparently. Signed off by Latchitt. Then again six months later.'

We peer at the scrawled signature next to the entries. It seems that whenever something dies in the animal house, it's a Latchitt who finds it. Not just spiders, either, there are all sorts in the log: stick insects, mice, birds . . .

'So maybe they didn't actually die,' I say. 'Maybe they were just moved somewhere else.'

In the quiet of the insect room, I hear something that makes every hair on my body stand on end. Gus grabs Naira's arm and turns towards the door.

'Did you hear that?'

The sound comes again – a whistled tune,

distant but clear, and getting louder. It's Mr Latchitt.

'We should hide,' Naira says. 'Maybe he doesn't know we're here.'

'We've switched all the lights on,' I say. 'He'll know.' I start looking around for escape routes. There are no doors other than the one we came in. There are windows big enough to squeeze through, but the animal house leads out on to the field, and that's the last place I want to go.

'There are four of us,' Hallie says. 'And one of him. We knock him out, steal his keys, and go get help. I'm going to look for a weapon.'

'But we don't know for sure that he's done anything wrong.' Naira takes the logbook that Hallie is waving around out of her hands. 'Imagine the trouble we'll be in if we attack the school groundskeeper.'

'She's right,' says Gus. 'There will be no coming back from that.'

'I'm eighty per cent sure he's evil,' Hallie says. 'I'm prepared to live with those odds.'

'Hal, we don't have a weapon, and there's no room in here for any of us to get behind him, or even swing a fist properly. It won't work.' We're full-on panicking now.

'I know!' Gus says. 'We release the crickets!'

'Why?' Naira asks.

'Classic distraction. Works every time.'

'We're not movie kids defending our home from burglars,' Hallie huffs, but Gus is already taking the lid off the box.

'Be free, my chirping friends!' He scatters them across the bench. 'Now we make it look like we've been here, but gone. We're twelve years old – leaving lights on in empty rooms is one of our life skills.'

The whistling is getting closer and closer. There's no time.

'Hide,' I say. 'Under the benches. Now.'

The creak of a door gives us the kick up the butt we need to move. There are piled-up books and boxes underneath the high benches that the tanks sit on. We slide them across and crawl into the dusty space behind them – Hallie and I on one side, Gus and Naira on the other. I settle myself as far back into the gap as I can, and try to be still. Just in time.

Mr Latchitt is in the mammal room. I hear his heavy footsteps, treading slowly as he passes the cages. If he knows we're there, he's in no hurry to find us. You'd think, seeing the lights on, he'd call out to ask if there's someone around. But he just whistles, that same tune – the one Mrs Latchitt was humming when she threw the chicken down the well.

He's into the aquatic room now, passing the Angelo fish and the axolotls. The crickets Gus let out are jumping around the bench, and some of them have landed on the floor. I hear the taps of their feet, and their soft chirruping as they skitter, then rest. As Mr Latchitt gets closer, I try to place the tune he's whistling. It's there, in the back of my mind – something I've heard a million times before but not really paid attention to. Scraps of words start to form in my head. I'm so close to remembering.

I can feel the answer tickling at my brain, as the door to the insect room creaks, and Mr Latchitt enters. He must see the crickets, but he doesn't react, which feels wrong. I mean, you'd swear, or step back, or grab the box, or do something. But he doesn't. Around the edge of the box I see his legs come into view. He's wearing dark work trousers, loose-fitting with loads of pockets, and marked with old stains. His boots are big, brown, heavy and laced up tight. Same as the trousers, they're worn, like they've been around for years. His long coat is dripping the last traces of rainwater on to the floor. There's a smell that's come in with him – a mix of rain, wood smoke, rotting leaves and something chemical: sharp and acidic.

A cricket hops across the aisle, landing on the ground right in front of Mr Latchitt. He stops. He's seen it – he must have. Then he raises his foot, slowly and carefully, and crushes the cricket under his boot, taking his time like he wants to enjoy the moment and savour the crunch. Hallie grabs my arm and grips it tight.

Mr Latchitt stops whistling for a moment, just as the words to the tune butterfly further to the front of my mind . . . something about rain and being washed away.

He lifts his foot, and I see the remains of the cricket smeared on the floor, some of it sticking to the boot and pulling away like green pizza cheese. Hallie has a pincer grip on my arm, squeezing so hard that the tips of my fingers start to tingle.

Another step forward. He's less than a metre away now – I could reach out and touch him if I wanted to. Obviously I don't. Everything is still and silent, except for the chatter of the crickets. Then suddenly there's a smash above our heads, like one of the tanks has exploded. Shards of glass rain down around us, skidding across the floor. Hallie practically rips my arm off, and I hear a squeak of surprise through the shower of glass, coming from where Gus and Naira are hiding. Did Mr Latchitt hear? There's a couple of seconds of painful waiting, and I ready myself to come out with an explanation, or to run, or even fight if I have to. But then there's another deafening smash, and another, and another, and another. Mr Latchitt's boots disappear out of view, the smashes coming loud and fast. Amongst the flying glass, there's dirt, and twigs, and leaf litter, and I realise that he's destroying all the insect tanks. Finally the smashes stop, the sound still ringing in my ears. Mr Latchitt's boots appear in front of us again, like he knows exactly where we are, then he turns and walks back towards the door. I hear the door close and a key turn in the lock. Then the click of a light switch plunges the room into thick black darkness. As Mr Latchitt leaves, he starts whistling again, and as the words finally come tsunami-ing in, it feels like my heart thuds to a stop.

Incy. Wincy. Spider.

CHAPTER NINE

BLIND

'Is anyone hurt?' I ask. My voice sounds too loud in the darkness, but then I figure it doesn't matter now. Mr Latchitt knows we're here.

'Nope,' says Hallie.

'No.' Naira.

'Only psychologically,' Gus says.

Hallie has loosened her grip on my arm slightly. 'Good to know that Mr Latchitt is as crazy as his wife.'

'Yeah,' I say. 'That tune he whistles. It's "Incy Wincy Spider".'

'Jesus,' Gus says.

My right leg is cramping so bad. I'm going to have to move soon. 'Well, we came here for answers and we got some,' I say. 'Just not the ones we wanted.'

'I have a question.' Naira's voice sounds shaky. 'Is that spider now loose in this room?'

'She'll be scared,' I say. 'She'll find somewhere quiet to hide. She's no threat . . .'

'But?' Gus says. 'You're going to say "but", I can tell.'

I sigh. 'It's some of the other creatures he set free in here that we need to be worried about.'

'Oh god,' Hallie says. 'This is bad.'

'Do I want to know what the other creatures are?' Naira asks. 'Actually, let me answer that for you – no, I don't want to know. I just want you to tell me how we're getting out of here without being scratched, bitten or stung.'

'You don't think the big one's in here, do you?' Gus says. 'He could have let it inside, couldn't he? I mean, that's possible.'

I stare into the black around me – it stretches outwards like an endless void. But it's not a void, is it? It's full of hidden dangers, some that I know about and maybe some that I don't. And now the shocked silence is broken by slight noises – the patter of hooked feet on the tiles; the tinkle of glass as something disturbs the debris and it falls off the bench above us; the vibration of tiny wings; a set of padded feet scuttling across the floor.

'They're making creepy bug noises,' Naira squeaks.

'Bugs do that,' I say. 'Except the spiders. They'll be silent.' Then I bite my lip because it wasn't the cleverest thing to say.

A sudden croaking sound in the space between us makes Naira scream. 'There's something on me. Get it off!' I hear a thud as she jumps up, forgetting that she's under a heavy wooden bench, but she ignores it and starts thrashing around, Gus trying to calm her. She's losing it. We need to do something now.

'The light switch is outside,' Hallie says to me. 'But I think I remember where the window is. If we can get to it and pull the blind up, we'll have some light at least.'

'Good plan,' I say. 'Let's do it.'

I pull the sleeves of my sweatshirt over my hands to give them some protection from the broken glass and anything else they might come across, and tell Hallie to do the same. Then we crawl out from behind the boxes, bumping into things I don't remember being there and generally making a mess of it.

'It's like one of those cartoons,' Hallie says. 'Where they step on a rake and it smacks them in the head, then they turn and put their foot on a landmine and their arm in a bear trap.'

I laugh, then wince, as a piece of glass cuts through my sweatshirt and into the palm of my hand. Then I laugh again.

Hallie laughs too. 'This is so not funny, Angelo.' There's a thump that sounds like human connecting with desk leg, and then,

'Damn it!' followed by giggling.

'I'm being punished,' Naira cries. 'For what I did. For cheating. This is my fault.'

'What are you talking about, Naira?' Gus says. 'You've never cheated at anything in your life – you're an A-star genius, you don't need to.'

'I did, though,' she says. 'You don't know.'

I wonder, mid-crawl, if I should ask her what she means, but to be honest we have bigger things to worry about right now.

'Guys, Naira is losing her shiz!' Gus calls.

'One minute,' I call back. 'We're going to get some light in.' I feel above me to make sure I'm not under the bench any more before I stand up. Something brushes my ear, making me jump, but I manage not to cry out. Naira is crying and has stopped responding to any of Gus's questions. We need to find a way out of here.

'There.' I hear Hallie's voice next to me. 'You see that faint bit of light? That must be it.'

We crunch through the glass towards the strip of dim light. At one point my foot comes down on something squashy that definitely isn't glass, but I try not to think about it. When we're underneath where the window must be, Hallie says, 'Boost me. I know where the string is to open it.' So I kneel down, clumsy as an elephant on a skateboard, and help Hallie climb up to the window. I hear scuffling and scraping, and then I hear the clack of the blind as it slowly rises.

Outside, the rain has stopped, but the sky is still charcoal-grey. The dregs of light that seep in are weak and depressing. But they're enough to reveal the carnage around us. The remains of the tanks are everywhere – the floor, walls and even the ceiling are spattered with mud and dirt. And the fragments of glass twinkle in the dull sunlight, coating every surface like a layer of razor snow.

'He didn't just smash up the room,' I say. 'He totally destroyed it.'

'Yeah, he swung like he meant it, for sure,' says Hallie.

'Do you think you can crawl out now?' I call over to Gus and Naira. 'I can't see anything in your path except glass and dirt.'

'We're coming,' Gus calls back after a pause, and then I hear the shuffle of boxes being slid out of the way, and first Gus, then Naira emerge from the gloom. Naira has her PE bottoms tucked into her socks, her sleeves pulled down to cover her hands, and her shoulders hunched up to protect her neck. Her face is red and puffy and she jumps at every tiny sound, and sometimes at nothing at all. I've never had that fear of insects that some people have, and never really understood it. Bugs and spiders are fascinating – going about their lives literally under our noses, playing out their own epic stories and doing loads for the environment without bothering us. But seeing Naira now, I realise her fear isn't something that's in her control – it's real to her, even if it's irrational.

Naira and Gus join us under the window, and I look around the room while I assess the situation.

'I need to get out of here,' Naira says. 'Can we break the door down?'

'It's a heavy door,' I say. 'And we have nothing we can use as a battering ram.'

'What about Hallie?' Gus says. 'I'll get her arms, you grab her legs, and we'll run her at it head first.'

'I'm up for that.' Hallie rubs her hands. 'Let's do it.'

'You actually would, wouldn't you?' Gus shakes his head. 'I was joking, you nutter.'

'Battering-ram me,' she says, bouncing on her toes. 'Come on, do it.'

'Hal, we're not battering-ramming you,' I say. 'That's insane.'

'We can find something to wrap around my head for padding.' She starts looking around for bubble wrap, or a pillow, or whatever it is she has in mind.

'All right, stand back,' Gus suddenly says, and then he charges at the door, throwing his shoulder at it with a surprising amount of force. The impact makes a loud crunch, but the sound comes from Gus's body, not the door, which stands there unbothered, looking at us all like we're morons as Gus bounces off it and falls back on to the floor.

'I'm fine,' Gus says through gritted teeth, picking himself up, tears in his eyes.

'What the hell?' Hallie says as we all stare at him with a mixture of confusion and respect.

'One of us was going to have to give it a go.' He shrugs, then winces. 'I thought I'd get it over with. Save us some time.'

Hallie gives herself a shake. 'My turn now – you probably loosened it, and another hit will bust it completely.'

'That's really nice of you to say, Hal,' Gus says. 'But it didn't flinch, even under my magnificent buffness. It's not going to work.'

'Are you saying I'm weaker because I'm a girl?'

'No, I'm saying that Dwayne Johnson could run at that door, and it would just knock him on his muscular butt and have a good laugh at him.'

'You don't know The Rock is stronger than me.' Hallie glares. 'Until I've fought him, no one can know for sure.'

'Can we focus on getting out of here, please?' Naira says.

'If it helps, Hallie, I'd rather have you on my team than The Rock,' I say, because she looks genuinely hurt. 'But Naira's right. We can't stay here – Mr Latchitt could come back at any time and it's clear that has no problem with us getting hurt . . .'

'. . . or eaten by spiders,' Gus says.

'He's probably planning to feed us to them,' Naira says.

Hallie nods. 'He's chickening us.'

'I know things are bad, but can we stop using nouns as verbs,' says Naira. 'It's unbearable.'

'And as the door isn't an option, our only choice is the window, a ventilation shaft, or digging an escape tunnel,' I say.

'Imagine being chased by a giant spider through a ventilation shaft.' Gus shudders.

'But the window leads out on to the field,' Naira shrieks. 'There's no way I'm going back on to that field.'

Hallie frowns. 'So we're left with digging a tunnel? How long's that going to take?'

'Too long,' I say. 'If Mr Latchitt comes back, he'll catch us for sure. I'm not excited about the thought of being underground, either.'

'Are you suggesting we drop out of the window and run?' Hallie asks.

'No.' I think back to that time I wanted to see into the ornamental gardens. 'I'm suggesting we climb out of the window and try to get up on the roof. It's low on this part of the science block. If we can pull ourselves up, we should be able to get on to the main roof of the block, where we'll have a good view of the field, and the Latchitts' house. We can plan our next move.'

'Right,' Gus says. 'Makes sense. And I'm famous for my incredible upper body strength, so climbing should be easy.'

'What do you guys think?' I look at Hallie and

Naira. We're a team, so everyone should get a say.

'Yeah,' says Hallie. 'Sounds good.'

'It does not sound good,' Naira huffs. 'But it's better than staying here.' And she grabs the end of the nearest bench. 'Help me with this, will you?'

We drag the bench across the floor and under the window. If Mr Latchitt comes back he'll be able to see where we exited, but hopefully he won't guess that we've gone up rather than down. I slide the window open. It groans and scrapes, but eventually there's a gap wide enough for us to fit through.

'I'll go first,' I say.

'Why do you get to go first?' Hallie asks. Of course she does.

'Because I've done it before,' I say, which makes the others raise their eyebrows. 'Don't ask me why – we don't have time for that right now. But I know I can do it, so I'll get up on to the animal-house roof and then I can help guide the rest of you, and give you a hand if you need it.'

'I hate to be negative,' Gus says, leaning out of the window and turning his head to look up. 'But I think I'm going to need it.'

'It's not as bad as it looks,' I say. 'The hardest part is getting yourself out without falling. There's only a small ledge to grip on to. But once you're out, there's a solid iron drainpipe to wrap your arms around and an alarm box to use as a foothold. The walls and the roof are uneven so you can get a good grip.'

'And if we fall . . .' Naira says.

'. . . it will be to certain death,' Hallie finishes. 'With a load of pain and terror to come before the end.'

'Good, then,' Gus says. 'I'm excited. Anyone else?'

The girls roll their eyes, and I take the opportunity to pull myself out of the window, before we can talk ourselves out of it.

CHAPTER TEN

UP

With the window ledge icy wet, and the wind battering at me, it's much harder to keep my grip than it was the last time I did this. I know I won't be able to hold on for long, so I need to move fast. I allow myself a second to take a breath, then push upwards from my toes and grab one of the bolts that holds the drainpipe to the wall, swinging there for a moment before my trainers find spots to dig in on, and I can get enough purchase to start pulling myself up. Once my arms are circled around the pipe, I edge upwards, as fast as I dare. Once I'm high enough to get my foot on the old security alarm box, all I have to do is push off to get the boost I need to be able to grab the edge of the roof. I manage it, not easily, but without disaster, which is probably as much as I can hope for on a day like today. Once I have a good grip on the roof, I heave myself over the edge.

I look down to where they're hanging out of the window. Naira should be able to make the climb without too much trouble – she's tall and athletic. It will be Hallie and Gus who struggle the most. I give them a wave and a grin. 'Who's next?' I shout as the wind whips around me and makes being on a roof seem like not the best idea.

I'm not surprised to see Hallie going for it next. It's like she always has a point to prove – that she's brave and tough and not afraid to take anyone on. It must be tiring living life like that, but maybe no more tiring than my technique of acting like I don't care about anything. She sits on the window ledge, back to the field, and stretches to grab the upper frame. Hallie's strong, but she's the shortest, so it's going to be hard for her to reach the hand and footholds. She shows no fear as she takes the plunge and stands up.

'You're going to have to jump a bit to reach the pipe,' I shout. 'Get your right arm around it and hang on. The wall is uneven so you should be able to steady yourself with your feet.'

She nods, and jumps. There's a heart-dropping moment when she slides down a few centimetres, but she recovers, and once she's on the pipe she makes solid progress. I lie on my stomach and reach down to help her up on to the roof. 'Easy,' she says, once she's sitting safely on the tiles, trying to get her breath back.

Gus goes next. He looks pale and afraid, but he doesn't hesitate, taking a deep breath and climbing out on to the ledge. A strong gust of wind powers into him, just as he's about to make the jump to the pipe. It rattles the window and his fingers slip. He tips backwards in a horrible slow-motion movement, a look of panic on his face. Hallie swears, and I reach out a hand to try to stop him falling, even though I'm too far away to have any chance. He sort of hovers mid-fall for a second or two, arms windmilling, stuck in a no man's land between saving himself and falling. But then an arm shoots out of the open window and grabs him by the front of his sweatshirt, yanking him inwards and sending him crashing face first into the glass. He gets his grip and hugs the wall for a few seconds, then looks up at us with a massive grin on his face. 'Lol!'

'Freaking hell, Gus!' Hallie shouts. 'I nearly peed myself.'

He smooshes his face into the window, planting a kiss on the surface. 'Thanks, Naira,' he shouts.

'Jesus,' I say. 'That was too close.'

Gus makes the rest of the climb without any further dramatic moments, and when he gets up to the roof, he just sits and laughs hysterically for a few minutes.

'That was messed up.' He wipes his eyes. 'I wish I had it on video.'

'This whole thing would make a good movie,' I say. 'If we survive this detention we should sell the story rights to Steven Spielberg or someone.'

We're watching Naira make the ascent carefully but easily.

'Yes!' Gus says. 'I will play myself, and The Rock can be my body-double.'

We laugh.

'Maybe I could get enough money to pay off our flat,' I say. 'Then my parents wouldn't have to work as much.' I smile at the thought of it. 'And I'd get my brother the newest console so he can play online with his friends.'

'What are we talking about?' Naira asks as we all give her a hand getting over the edge of the roof. Not that she needs it.

'Before we talk, we should move further into the centre,' I say, pointing to the main science-block roof, which is an easy climb up stepped tiles. They look slippery from the rain, but the wind has dropped, and the sun breaks through for a moment, making me squint as I look out over the grounds. 'You can see across the whole field from there.'

'And the Latchitts?' Hallie asks.

'Yep,' I say. 'We should be able to see them moving around the grounds, and if they do know we're here and decide to come up to the roof for us, we'll see them coming.'

'Do you think we'll be able to stay up here?' Hallie asks as we start climbing the gentle slope to the main roof. 'It's a good spot for defending our position. We can push them down if they try to climb up. And we're far away from whatever's under the ground.'

'The problem is, we don't know how long it'll be,' I say. 'The detention goes on till two thirty, right?'

'Yeah,' Gus says. 'Then our parents will know something's up.'

'Anyone's parents picking them up? Or were you all planning on walking home?' I ask.

'Walking,' Hallie says.

'Me too.' Naira.

'And me.' Gus.

'So there's probably going to be another hour after the end of detention before they get worried,' I say.

'Then my mum will go mental,' Naira says. 'She'll be climbing the gates to find me.'

'And do you really want her to be coming in here?' I say. Because I've thought about this. I mean, no one's going to come looking for me for ages, but if they did . . .

'Oh god,' Naira says, as she realises.

'And we can't warn anyone,' says Hallie.

'If they come here, they could end up lost underground,' Gus says. 'Or dead.'

We reach the rough centre of the roof where there's a large metal box rising up. It has a grill on top, and under its slats there's a rusted fan the size of a tyre. From this point you can see nearly the entire school in a way that makes it almost beautiful. Everything looks different from above. The field is wide and green, and lined with late-autumn trees, finches perched in the upper branches looking out over everything just like we are. I often think how amazing it would be to be able to grow wings and fly away. Away from the lessons and the never-ending rules. Away from the noise and the corridor crush. Away from nagging teachers trying to make you write poetry. I see the smoke still curling from the Latchitts' chimney, but there's no sign of anyone or anything else moving around.

'We can cover all angles from here,' I say. 'Let's sit while we work out how the hell we're going to get out of this.'

We settle down on to the roof, each of us leaning up against one side of the metal vent so we can see in every direction, but we can't see each other. I roll my shoulders back, feeling the strain of the climb across my upper back, and stretch out my legs. I feel the rainwater soaking through my tracksuit bottoms again, and those minutes of sitting warm on the classroom floor seem like hours ago.

'So what were you talking about earlier?' Naira asks again.

'Angelo was telling us about all the selfish things he's going to spend his movie money on,' Gus snorts.

'What movie money?' Naira asks.

'The movie of us and this.' Hallie indicates the roof, the field, the Latchitts' house and everything else around us. '*The Dread Wood High Massacre.*'

'We're not dead yet,' I say.

'And I have no intention of dying,' Naira says, apparently more like her old self now that she's not trapped in a room with a bunch of snakes and spiders. 'I have too much to do. There's GCSEs, A levels, university . . .'

'Do you measure your life in exams?' Gus looks at her in bewilderment.

'No,' she says. 'I see it as a series of opportunities to achieve my goals, so that I can go on and be a barrister, live in a nice house, and look after my mum when she's old.'

'How is it even possible that you ended up in detention?' Hallie says.

'I've been thinking about that, actually,' Naira says. 'And it's something we should probably talk about.'

It's like my heart squirms with worms, twisting in my chest, making vomit rise up from my belly. I don't want to talk about this, and I'm glad the others can't see my face.

'Shouldn't we focus on the Latchitts? And the spiders?' Gus says, his voice sounding full of something like nerves, or fear maybe.

'Yeah, I agree,' Hallie says in her usual bold way, but it feels forced. 'We need to work out what we're going to do next.'

There's a moment where we all say nothing, and I genuinely don't know what anyone else is thinking. The sky darkens again, and it looks like either the storm is returning, or a new one is breaking through. I don't know which is worse.

'Heads up,' Gus says. 'Something's happening at the Latchitts' house.'

'Do you have eyes on one of them?' I ask, staying put for now in case the activity is a distraction so that we're not watching our backs.

'Both of them,' Gus answers. 'They're both in the yard, and it looks like they're . . .' He pauses. 'You guys should see this.'

CHAPTER ELEVEN

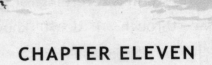

CARNAGE

I figure if both Latchitts are in view, we don't have to worry about one of them sneaking up on us. So I shuffle around the vent and sit next to Gus, Hallie and Naira, looking out beyond the field. Mr and Mrs Latchitt are walking down their back garden path – the same route that Mrs Latchitt took when I watched her through the fence what feels like hours ago – both carrying what looks like brown fabric in their hands. I can't hear them over the wind and the distance, but from the look of Mr Latchitt's mouth, I'd say he was whistling.

'It's "Incy Wincy Spider",' I say. 'The tune he whistles and Mrs Latchitt hums.'

'That is dark,' Gus agrees.

'Yeah,' I say.

'Wait, how does it go again?' Hallie asks. 'We used to sing it in nursery, I think. There was some weird thing we did with our fingers while we sang.'

'Like this.' Naira demonstrates: touching the pad of her thumb on her right hand to the tip of her left index finger, then twisting her hands to alternate them. She moves them upwards. She sings the song as she does it, and we all listen in silence.

'Well, I think we've found the one thing you're not good at,' Gus says. 'I hope you weren't planning to take part in a talent show.'

We all snigger, and Naira whacks Gus in the arm.

'Are they doing what I think they're doing?' Hallie asks, turning our full attention back to the Latchitts.

The cloths they're holding are sacks – the rough brown kind that lots of the pig supplies come in. I've seen them stacked in the storehouse in the yard before. They're large, and tough, good for carrying heavy things because they don't rip easily. Mrs Latchitt has opened one of the henhouses and is merrily dragging the chickens out and stuffing them into a sack that Mr Latchitt is holding open. The chickens struggle and wisps of feather flutter off in the wind.

'It's not looking good for those chickens,' I say as the first sack fills up. Mr Latchitt ties it round the neck with a bit of rope and then they move on to filling the second sack.

'They don't seem to be wishing-welling them, though,' Hallie says. 'So that's a good sign, right?'

'Let's not get our hopes up, Hal,' says Gus. 'I don't think they're moving them into a luxurious new chicken mansion.'

'Poor things, they must be so scared,' Hallie says.

'Can chickens be scared?' Naira asks. 'Genuine question.'

'Of course they can,' Hallie snaps back. 'Animals have feelings, Naira.'

'Yes, I'm sure some animals do,' Naira says. 'But I just don't see it with chickens.'

'The question we should really be asking,' Gus says as the Latchitts finish stuffing the sacks and head to their back gate that leads on to the field, 'is can chickens fly? I mean, they're birds, right? But you never see them flying.'

'They can fly a bit,' I say. 'But only with a few metres of height, and not very far. It's more like a big, flappy jump.'

The Latchitts are on the field now, each carrying a writhing bag. About twenty metres in, they stop and untie their sacks, the wind buffeting their clothes. Then Mr Latchitt kisses his wife on the cheek, and they split up, him heading towards the pig yard, and her continuing the route closer to the school buildings.

'You think they know we're here?' Gus says. Our eyes are fixed on the Latchitts, waiting to see what they'll do next.

'Surely they think we're still locked in bug city,' Naira says. 'Or if they went back to check, and noticed the open window, they'll think we're down there somewhere.'

'Maybe they're going in different directions because they're looking for us,' Hallie says. 'Should we lie flat, in case they look up here? So they're less likely to spot us?'

'Yeah,' I say, with a growing feeling of dread. 'I wouldn't mind getting a bit closer too. We might notice something useful, or at least be able to hear Mrs Latchitt. She's moving her lips, see?'

We manoeuvre ourselves around as smoothly and noiselessly as possible, until we're all lying on our stomachs, then we wiggle forward.

'I feel like a commando,' Gus whispers, using his elbows to push himself over the tiles.

'Gus, this is no time to talk about your

pants,' Hallie tuts. 'I really don't want to hear about your underwear preferences.'

'Ew,' Naira says. 'Hallie, stop.'

'Guys, I said "a commando", not "going commando". You have inappropriate minds.'

'Oops,' whispers Hallie. 'Sorry, Gus.'

'And for your information, I wear very classy pants.'

'No need, Gus,' Naira says, while I bite my lip so I won't laugh out loud.

As we get closer to Mrs Latchitt, I hear her voice drifting up to our hiding place. 'She's singing,' I say. 'Their favourite song.'

We listen for a few seconds. 'She's better than Naira,' Gus says, getting an elbow in the ribs as a result.

'Why, though?' Hallie says.

'Because Naira's voice is like squeaky sneakers on a gym floor,' says Gus.

'No, I meant why are they always singing and whistling that tune? I get that they're creepy, and that they want to freak us out,' Hallie says. 'But don't you think there might be another reason for it? Something we don't know about?'

'Like what?' Naira asks.

'Earworm,' Gus says. 'They have a pet spider, so it pops in their heads and then they can't get rid of it.'

'Maybe,' I say, but I'm thinking Hallie is right. I don't think the Latchitts do anything without a reason.

Mrs Latchitt is literally skipping across the grass like a toddler, singing her nursery rhyme like she's on her way to a picnic. Her hair is tied under a scarf, but some of her grey curls have escaped and are bouncing about in the breeze. Every now and then a huge gust blows, making us grip the roof tighter in case we blow away. But she carries on her way like she doesn't have a care in the world, the sack swinging by her side. She's clasping it tight to make sure it doesn't fall open now that it's untied.

140

Mr Latchitt is striding slowly but purposefully in a parallel line to her but at the back of the field, past the Dread Wood. He's serious and steady, in contrast to her prancing, but they keep pace with each other, even being maybe fifty metres apart. I look from one to the other, trying to decide which of them is worse.

As Mrs Latchitt gets closer to where we're watching from the roof, we shrink down as much as we can. Our navy PE kits don't exactly blend with the grey and brown of the roof, but there's no reason why she should see us from so far below.

She's just a few metres from the animal house, when she stops suddenly, at the exact moment that Mr Latchitt stops just ahead of the pig yard.

'Couple goals,' Hallie whispers.

Then Mr Latchitt reaches into his sack, pulls out a chicken and launches it across the grass. It flaps and falls in a feathery mess, but lands on its feet and takes a few wobbly steps forward.

For once none of us have anything to say. We just watch. The chicken recovers enough to start pecking the ground in front of it, milling about, looking for food. A strong rush of wind makes it jump and attempt a mini flight, landing a couple of metres further away from Mr Latchitt. It bobs around again, moving this way and that. Everyone else – the four of us and the Latchitts – stays completely still. I'm aware of pieces of grit on the roof digging into my arms, and the backs of my still damp tracksuit bottoms sticking to my legs. The air smells of nothing but cold and wet, and it stings the inside of my nose, making it start to run. I scan the ground around the chicken, looking for any shifts or tremors, but we're far enough away, and the wind is lashing the grass so much that I can't see. I glue my eyes to the chicken, straining to keep them open. If I blink I could miss something. I need to see.

And then it happens. The earth by the chicken rises to reveal a hidden hole, the grassy lid lifting just enough for a pair of legs the thickness of my forearms to dart out, grabbing the chicken and pulling it down into the burrow. Then the lid drops, and the field looks just as it did before the chicken even existed.

'Spider,' I hiss at the others. Because they must all have seen those legs and know that they didn't belong to a human. 'Massive trapdoor spider.'

None of them say anything back – I think they're in shock.

Mrs Latchitt whoops and cackles with laughter while Mr Latchitt reaches into his sack and tosses out the rest of the chickens – three of them – one by one. Then he strides across to the pig yard, walking right over the concealed burrow without fear, without flinching, like he knows he's in no danger. Then he sits on the wall that encloses the yard, crosses his legs and pulls a foil package out of one of the deep pockets in his trousers. He carefully unwraps it to reveal a sandwich – thick wedges of crusty bread filled thickly with stuff I can't see from this distance. He picks it up and takes a bite, screwing up the foil with his other hand and returning it to his pocket. Then he sits there slowly chewing, while the chickens strut around the field.

'What the actual?' Hallie hisses.

One of them disappears in a cloud of feathers around the spot where Mr Canton went under. So quick I don't even get a glimpse of spider.

Mrs Latchitt claps her hands. Mr Latchitt takes another bite of sandwich.

The next chicken makes it almost to the wall where Mr Latchitt is sitting before the ground opens up underneath it. Two legs grab for it, dark grey and covered in bristles, clearly visible against the bright green grass. The chicken jumps, flaps its wings, makes an attempt to fly out of reach. I hear the others gasp as two more legs appear and the four legs work as a team, latching on to the chicken, tugging and twisting it, and pulling it downwards.

'Those legs, though,' Hallie gasps.

'I can't believe I'm saying this,' Naira whispers. 'But that is, for sure, a monster spider.'

'Yeah,' Gus says. 'Spider-zilla.'

The chicken makes a surprise comeback, scratching and jabbing.

'Go on, son,' Gus says as it squawks and pecks, getting a bit of air before another leg pulls it back down.

'You realise chickens are all girls, right?' Hallie whispers.

'Then how do they make baby chickens?' Gus whispers back.

'Shush,' Naira says.

The chicken lasts a few seconds more, then is dragged underground. The last one is walking back towards the Dread Wood, when Mrs Latchitt puts her arm into her sack and takes out another one. She pats it on the head, then throws it into the air. It lands in a heap and is gone before it can even right itself. She giggles and tips the other two out by her feet, humming and swaying as they swagger around her, staying close.

'It's like they trust her,' I whisper.

'Off you go, sweetlings,' she says, shooing them away. One of them trots off, but the other remains by her feet, so she swings back her leg and gives it a swift kick, sending it flying.

Hallie lets out a tiny squeak, and I turn my head to see her biting her own hand. She looks stricken. I lean in to her slightly, to give her a supportive nudge. I mean, it's shocking to watch – especially when you can't do anything about it. But I saw Hallie earlier with the pigs. She really loves them, and values animals like they're people. I'm surprised she hasn't leaped off the roof to punch Mrs Latchitt in the face, and I know it's taking a lot of willpower for her to quietly watch.

One by one, the chickens are taken. Each

one from a different spot on the field. My breath catches in my throat, and my heart pounds. I try to wrap my head around it. There is an enormous spider living under our school field. And it's clear that this spider is happy to hunt as long as there's prey to be caught. Its burrows must run across all of the Dread Wood grounds. Nowhere is safe.

When the field is still again, Mr Latchitt finishes the last bite of his sandwich and heads into the pig yard.

'No,' Hallie says. 'Please, no.'

He pulls the gate wide and props it open, then takes a bucket of pig feed from the storage area and scatters it in a trail from the sty, to the gate, then out on to the field. He puts the bucket away and then opens the sty.

Mrs Latchitt hums and hopscotches across the stretch of field in front of our hiding place, like there's an invisible grid. Back and forth, humming and giggling, like she's just watched a West End show rather than a chicken genocide.

Mr Latchitt leaves the pig yard, with all the gates open and the food trail of horror snaking towards an unspeakable death, and then crosses the field to Mrs Latchitt. I hear his whistling get louder as he comes close, the tune slower than I would sing it – almost leisurely, like his walk. When he reaches Mrs Latchitt, she stops hopscotching and takes his hand, looking up at him with a beaming smile.

Then they both turn, look straight up to where we're hiding, Mrs Latchitt's eyes meeting mine for the second time today, and they raise their hands and wave.

CHAPTER TWELVE

MINEFIELD

We all gasp and jerk backwards, an instinctive defensive move that's not going to change the fact that the Latchitts know exactly where we are, and apparently have done all along.

Mrs Latchitt giggles. 'I always win at hide-and-seek, sweetlings.'

Then they turn and walk, hand in hand, back towards their cottage. None of us say anything until we've watched them let themselves back into their yard through the gate at the edge of the Dread Wood, and go inside the house.

'So this is worse than we thought,' Gus says. 'And we thought it was pretty freaking bad.'

'Apparently they are actual psychopaths.' I rub my face with my knuckles. I don't get scared easily, and I don't want to freak the others out, but it's hit home that we're in the middle of an unusually messed-up situation.

'We're in real trouble, aren't we?' Naira blinks, and I can see she has tears in her eyes. 'And there's no one around to help us.'

'I knew I should have kept my phone.' Hallie is looking around her, frantic, like her mobile might suddenly appear out of nowhere. 'Didn't I say there might be an emergency?'

'This is crazy. Kids don't end up in situations like this in real life. They just don't.' Gus looks like he's going to puke again.

We're all talking at once. Not listening to each other. Panicking. All of us lost in our own fear. I realise it's not going to help.

'Guys,' I say, but they don't seem to hear me. Naira is looking out towards the distant main road, waving her arms and jumping around to try to get someone's attention. Hal is trying to peel the tiles off the roof with her bare hands. Gus has gone completely still and silent. 'Guys!' I shout. 'I know this is a bad situation, but if we're going to get out of it, we need to stop and calm down.'

And they do stop. They all look at me, and I wonder how I managed to become the person that everyone looks at.

'We need to plan,' I say. 'We're not safe here. The Latchitts have been a step ahead of us the whole time. We need to do something instead of being herded around the school so that we're exactly where they want us.'

'You think they deliberately led us here?' Gus asks.

'I do,' I say.

'And what was that just now?' Naira asks. 'What was the point of sending all those chickens to their deaths?'

'That was a show,' I say. 'A show for our benefit.

They want us to know what they can do.'

'They want us to be terrified,' Hallie says. 'And I'm not playing their twisted games. They're sick. Both of them. No more hiding, we need to start sorting this shiz out.'

'Hold on, Hallie,' Naira says. 'We need to think about what we're doing. They're dangerous, and clever, and we can't go bombing around without planning first – we'll just make things worse.'

'How could things be worse?' Hallie shouts.

'We could be the chickens,' Gus says.

'Did you see the size of those spider legs?' Naira shouts back. 'How can that even be possible?'

'It's not,' I say. 'It's not possible. It must be the size of a dog. Even with the right conditions, it wouldn't grow that big. The Latchitts must have done something to it.'

'Something like what?' Gus asks.

Hallie's standing up now, pacing the roof, anger coming off her like an electromagnetic field.

'I don't know – something genetic?' I say, shrugging.

'If you don't know, Sir David Attenborough, then none of the rest of us will,' Naira snaps. 'We need to find out more about the Latchitts if we're going to get any answers.'

'How did it move under the field so fast?' Gus still looks totally confused. 'To the exact spots where the chickens were? X-ray eyes?'

'They weave a network of silk strands so that everything is connected,' I say. 'When something lands on the ground, the strands move slightly and they feel the vibrations.' I watch Gus's brain ticking away as he tries to take this in. 'But the speed it needed to move between the trapdoors that fast is insane. It shouldn't be possible. And what I really want to know is why it doesn't attack the Latchitts.'

'No!' Hallie shouts from a few metres away. She's looking over the field to the pig yard where Candace is venturing out of the sty, snuffling at the trail of food with her snout.

'Go back, Candace!' she screams. 'Guys, make loads of noise. Maybe we can frighten her into going back inside.'

We all stand and make as much of a commotion as we can: jumping, waving and yelling till our throats hurt. It achieves nothing. We stand and watch as she follows the trail, slowly making her way closer to the open gate of the yard.

'Nah,' Hallie says, pushing her sleeves up and looking over the edge of the roof. 'I'm not having it.'

'Not having what?' I ask, though I have a bad feeling about what she's going to do.

But Hallie is already swinging her leg down on to the alarm box. I reach forward to grab her, but realise I could knock her off balance. If she falls and lands badly, she'll have no chance of getting away if she's attacked.

'What the hell's she doing?' Naira shrieks.

'She's going for Candace,' I say, my brain speed-flicking through my options.

'Has she completely lost her mind?' Naira says.

But Hallie is already most of the way down the pipe. She doesn't hesitate. She hits the ground running, and storms on to the field, zigzagging and making sudden leaps. She avoids the spots where patches of chicken feathers are a helpful marker of the location of the hidden burrows. She's keeping her knees high and moving fast.

'She's thought this through,' I say, understanding her thinking. Mr Canton and the chickens were all moving slowly when they were attacked. She's going as fast as she can, and changing direction so the spider can't predict her direction and head her off.

'And she still did it anyway?' Gus shakes his head.

'Gotta admire her courage,' I say.

'You say courage, I say stupidity,' Naira says, but in a way that makes me think she's more impressed than she's letting on.

'The risky bit will be when she gets to Candace,' I say. 'The spider could be right there already. She'll have to slow down to grab her and get her back in the sty.'

I watch Hallie, halfway across the field now, and make my mind up. 'I'm going to help,' I say, and I'm off the roof in three seconds, using the toes of my trainers to control my slide down the drainpipe and feeling my nervous energy grow as I get closer to the ground. I touch down with a soft thud and then spring forward. Cold water seeps into my trainers as I run, soaking my socks up to my ankles. I try to make my movements unpredictable without losing speed, as I head across the field.

'Angelo!' I hear Naira shout from behind me, but I ignore it.

I've run fast a lot of times, for sport, for fun, and to get away from trouble. But this is something else. This is running for my life. I keep my eyes on the ground just ahead of me, looking for mounds and dips. If I stumble and fall, or if I slip on the wet grass, I'll be finished. Everything around me becomes a blur, as my ears fill with the sound of my own heavy breathing, and sweat starts to form on my face and back. Every second I expect the ground to open up, or to be yanked from behind by hairy legs. My entire body is on edge.

I glance up to see that Candace has left the yard and is trotting on to the grass, looking up at the sky with that smile on her face. And Klaus is following her, apparently able to sense-read the deepest secrets of my heart, but not the monster spider lurking under his trotters. Hallie's almost there, but she's going to have a choice to make. She'll struggle to carry one piglet, even with the adrenalin boost surging through her. She can't carry two.

I'm thirty metres away.

Hallie's almost there, and she's noticed the second piglet. She hesitates, trying to make a decision. I see the smallest quiver in the earth close to Candace.

Fifteen metres away.

Hallie shoots towards Candace, and I yell out, trying to warn her. I forget zigzagging and pelt straight at her, willing my arms and legs to move faster, knowing that every second could mean the difference between me being able to help, or me watching like an idiot as someone else gets dragged beneath the field. Mr Canton's horrified face flashes into my mind. His hands reaching for mine. The terror in his eyes. The earth piling on top of him as he was buried without a trace.

Five metres away.

Hallie reaches down to scoop up Candace at the exact same moment that a circle of earth rises, and two legs shoot towards the piglet too. They're thick as scaffold, and I can see that they're more brown than grey now that I'm close. Hallie doesn't stop to look – she was prepared for this. She skids to the ground, wrapping both arms around Candace, pulling her back with all she has. But the spider is stronger than she's expecting. It loosens its clutch for less than a second, so that it can rearrange its legs for a better grip. It grabs Candace, and Hallie with her, and yanks them towards the hole.

Two metres away.

But Hallie's a scrapper. Some people fight like they're performing a dance – skill and poise and seamless movements. Others are all teeth and nails and fists full of hair, lost to everything except the need to win. Hallie fights like nothing else matters. She kicks out hard, connecting with a part of the spider that I can't see yet. It recoils, but just for a second. More legs appear, moving lightning fast, catching Hal's ankle and wrenching it towards the tunnel.

I throw my weight on the lid of earth that covers the spider's torso, forcing it back down into the ground, only the tips of its legs caught in the rim of the lid. They're like nothing I've ever seen – covered in spiny hairs and clawed at the ends. Hallie pulls her legs away from the hole, just as an enormous force from below raises the lid again, throwing me off and sprawling on to the field, droplets of water from the soaking grass raining down on me. I turn to see the spider half emerged from its hole, revealing its head and the top part of its abdomen. And the size of it – the size of it blows my mind. It's impossibly big – its head the size of a basketball. And I'm struck by the hugeness of its eyes. Trapdoor spiders don't need the biggest eyes because they live underground and see by feeling. But these are powerful eyes – eyes that could be used for stalking, more like the ones you see on a jumping spider. That can't be good, and it crosses my mind that the Latchitts have done more than just provide extra oxygen to this animal.

Hallie kicks out again, her foot connecting with one of the spider's knee joints. It squeals and pulls back again – not totally, it's regrouping rather than retreating – giving Hal the time to get to her feet, a shocked Candace still in her arms. She backs away from the hole and turns to look for Klaus.

'Go,' I say. 'Take Candace. I'll get Klaus.'

She pauses. The spider lunges at her. But either it doesn't want to completely leave its burrow or it's decided there's easier prey because as Hallie takes another leap backwards, it apparently gives up and backs into the hole, the lid snapping shut behind it.

'You can't carry them both,' I say, picking myself off the ground. 'I'll get him.'

She nods and speeds off towards the pig yard, and I turn to look for Klaus. I spot him as far into the middle of the field as you would not want him to be, running on his little trotters like his life depends on it, which it probably does. I don't have time to waste thinking, so I speed after him, knowing that somewhere under my feet, the spider is doing the same thing.

CHAPTER THIRTEEN

LEG-TO-LEG COMBAT

I'm desperate to look behind me to make sure Hallie's made it to the sty with Candace, but I know it will slow me down. Instead I focus on Klaus. He's scared, so he's still running surprisingly fast in the opposite direction. He's the kindness pig, and it suits him; he can read my feelings like no human can. He's the first to come and nuzzle my hand when I visit the pig yard feeling frustrated or sad. There have been lots of times when hanging with him for twenty minutes has helped me get through the rest of the day. I never really appreciated it until this moment, when if I'm too slow, or if I trip, or if I lose my courage, he'll be gone.

I pick my way through the minefield. There are places that I know to avoid, but those are the easy ones. There could be hundreds more tunnels and trapdoors. Every time I plant my foot, I brace myself for disaster. And as I'm darting across the field, which is enormous, I wonder again how it was possible for the spider to get to each of the chickens so fast. Usually a spider has only one trapdoor, not loads of them dotted around a large area. And then there were those legs, which looked grey from a distance and brown close up . . . A new fear starts jabbing at my brain that maybe I've underestimated the situation.

The rain has started again. A mass of fine droplets fill the air, clinging to my eyelashes then dropping down into my eyes, making my vision blurred. I don't notice a rogue mound of tufted grass, and my toe catches it, sending me lurching forward. I manage to keep myself upright, but I've lost my stride and my breath. I picture the spider in its dark runs below me, gaining ground, lunging ahead. Will it reach Klaus before I get to him? Or will it lie in wait for me, springing up with no warning, and dragging me under the soil? I wonder what happens when it gets you. A bite first, most likely, to release toxins into your body, paralysing you. Then it probably wraps you in silk, stores you for later, secured on a tunnel wall, while the enzymes in its toxin slowly turn your insides into soup. I wonder what that feels like.

Klaus is slowing now, either worn out or thinking he's far enough away from the danger to be safe. His spotted butt is in my sights, just five metres or so away. And behind him, so quietly that he doesn't even turn his head, the ground starts to quiver.

The lid of earth rises slowly, revealing the hulking figure of the spider below. It emerges above the surface until three quarters of its body are visible. It's the darkest brown – the colour of the nasty chocolates that always get left in the box, then thrown away after Christmas. Its body is about a third larger than its basketball head, which makes me think it must be a male. A female's abdomen would be bigger – maybe double the size. Its eyes wrap around its face. Like jumping spiders it has two central eyes that are larger than the others. They're black, and shiny, and I swear they're looking at me.

It rears up like a cowboy horse in a western, its front legs raised, and I wait to see what it will do. That's when I realise it's waiting too. It hasn't decided what move it's going to make, yet. This is my chance. On my next stride, I place my right foot firmly, bend my knee and push up with as much force as I can. I'm aiming for something between a long jump and a high jump. I need enough air to get above the spider, but I also need to cover the distance – I'll only get one shot at this. I land with my left foot in the centre of the lid, and use it as a booster, to propel me further. I expect the jolt of my weight to maybe send the spider falling back down into the tunnel, but it hardly gives. This creature is strong. I try to keep my balance as I land, bending down to scoop up Klaus and tuck him under my left arm. He squeaks in surprise, and wriggles, making me half drop him. I have to stop to grab him with both hands, and in that split second of delay, I feel something grab my foot.

I instantly kick out, but it doesn't let go. It yanks me hard, and I crash to the ground, the sound of thunder roaring in my ears. Klaus slips out of my hands and I can't get any purchase on the drenched turf to pull myself towards him. As I lie on my belly, being dragged backwards, I see Klaus tearing away again, and honestly it makes me feel like crying. I put all my frustration into another kick, but the angle and the way the spider is gripping me mean my foot doesn't even make contact. I manage to turn my head enough to get a good look at it.

It's mostly out of its burrow, but it's holding the lid open with the ends of two of its back legs – just keeping that contact with the opening, and unwilling to let it go. If I can get just a bit further away, I'll be out of reach. I mean, I know it will pop up somewhere else, but at least I'll have a chance. I twist my body and kick with both feet, trying to loosen its grip. But it fights back, yanking and grappling until it gets a second grip further up the calf of my leg. It pulls, like it's barely even trying, managing to force me maybe half a metre closer to its burrow.

I'm scared now. More scared than I've ever been in my life. But I'm not going to give up – I'll fight for as long as I'm able. So I kick, again and again, refusing to lie still, flipping and jerking my body like a fish on a boat deck. I somehow roll myself on to my back, so I can see right into its eyes.

'Get the hell off me,' I shout. 'I'm not going in your nasty-ass tunnel.' I kick, getting a glancing blow off its face. 'I'm not having my insides turned to mush.' I kick again. 'I'm not letting you store me underground so you can drink me like soup. My brother needs me.' I kick again, and again, and again, with everything I have.

Then something huge suddenly looms into view from behind the earth lid. A shadow falls over me, and I hear a crunch. The spider drops me, bucking up again, its front legs waving. It roars in pain, then scuttles backwards into its hole, pulling the lid down behind it. On top of the lid, there's something green, and mechanical. It takes me a moment to put the details together in my messed-up mind.

'That's the most I've ever heard you say,' a voice calls out. 'And it was to a man-eating spider. I have to tell you, my feelings are hurt.'

A face smiles down at me through a blur of rain.

'Gus,' I say, and the word 'relief' isn't big enough to cover how I feel right now. He's on the ride-on mower, and he's using it to hold down the spider flap.

'Jump on,' he says, looking like a bad-A in shining armour. 'I'll carry you to safety.'

I stand and step up to the mower. It's a beast, wide tyres and thick metal casing. It must weigh two hundred and fifty kilos. Gus is perched on the only seat available. I go to get on behind him, but there's literally nowhere to put myself.

'You'll have to sit on my lap,' Gus grins.

'You're kidding,' I say.

He pats his thigh. 'It's either this or being a spider snack.'

I'm tempted to risk the spider for a second, but realise that would be ridiculous, so I climb up and lower myself on to Gus's lap.

'You see, that's not so bad, is it?' he says, putting his arms either side of me to grab the steering wheel. Then he steps on the gas,

169

sending us jolting forward.

'To the pigsty!' he whoops.

'Let's get Klaus first,' I say, pointing to where the piglet's finally stopped running and is sitting on the grass.

'To the pigsty, via Klaus!' Gus drives us forward at top speed, which is about fifteen miles per hour, and we slowly – painfully slowly – pootle across the field. When we reach Klaus, I jump down, gently pick him up, and then put him on my lap as we head back to the pig yard. He's heavy for a little pig.

Naira and Hallie are watching from the safety of the sty, the expressions on their faces strongly suggesting that we don't look as much like the heroes that Gus seems to think we are.

'Look at the girls,' Gus says. 'Checking us out.'

We bounce towards them over the mud. Me on Gus's lap, and Klaus on mine – an uncomfortable pile of survivors. I watch the girls' faces grow slowly bigger and bigger, as we take what feels like twenty minutes to chug towards them. Naira is flushed, her ponytail off-centre. Hallie is spattered with mud, her hair coming loose from her braids. They're both trying not to laugh.

'Can't we go any faster?' I say, feeling my face burn.

'This is top speed,' Gus says, patting the steering wheel with pride. 'We are bombing across this field, Angelo. Zooming. Hurtling. Practically flying. What a rush.'

By the time we reach the entrance to the pig yard, the girls have given up trying not to laugh, and are absolutely howling. I can't help but laugh too as we pull up outside the storage shed and I plop on to the yard, with Klaus tucked into my sweatshirt.

Gus turns off the ignition and slides down, looking like he just saved the world. He turns and strokes the bonnet. 'Rest well, my beauty,' he whispers, which makes us laugh harder.

'What?' he says, turning to us, arms out,

palms up.

I settle Klaus back into the sty with Candace, Reggie and Theo, the fresh, dry straw looking surprisingly cosy. I could honestly just curl myself up in it, snuggling with the pigs, and sleep. But instead I close the gate to the sty, making sure it's fastened securely, and face the others.

'We need to talk,' Naira says, like the rest of us are in serious trouble for something we can't remember doing.

'And I've got to sit down for a bit,' says Hallie. 'I'm done.'

'We need to be somewhere the spiders can't get us, and where we can keep a lookout too,' I say. I'm longing to get out of the rain, but we need to be watching our backs. We can't rest yet.

'So we go up again?' Gus points at the roof of the pigsty.

'Yeah.' I nod. 'We go up.'

CHAPTER FOURTEEN

WHAT HAPPENED THAT DAY . . . .

The pigsty roof is low, and we climb on to it easily. I'd prefer we had somewhere higher so that we could see more, but this is the best we're going to get without running back across the field, and I don't think any of us have the energy for that. The pigsty is built on a huge concrete slab, so there's no chance of anything burrowing up underneath us. We should be safe here.

'First of all,' Naira says. Apparently she's taking control of this conversation. 'What the hell were you thinking, Hallie? You could have been killed, and Angelo too.'

'I couldn't stand by and watch any more,' she says. 'And I flipping love those pigs.'

'More than you value your own life?' Gus asks.

Hallie shrugs.

'Would it have been worth it?' he says. 'Sacrificing your own life for a pig?'

'I guess we can only ask ourselves what kind of people we'd be if we left them to die,' I say.

'The same kind of people who watched a whole flock of chickens die without doing anything about it,' Gus says. 'I mean, there are lines drawn here that I'm not quite grasping. What makes a pig worth more than a chicken?'

'They're our friends,' Hallie says. 'We didn't know the chickens.'

'The chickens could have been brilliant people,' Gus says. 'And now they'll never get the chance to show you.'

'I didn't see you racing to save them,' says Hallie.

'Yeah, but I didn't race to save the pigs, either. Naira and I only came when we saw you two were getting in trouble.'

'Could've handled it myself,' Hallie huffs.

'But thank you from me,' I add quickly. 'Because I wasn't handling it as well as I would have liked. That spider – it isn't normal.'

They all roll their eyes. 'No shiz, man,' Gus says. 'It's the size of a hippo.'

'It is not the size of a hippo,' Naira says. 'Exaggerating isn't going to help us.'

'I meant a pygmy hippo, actually,' Gus sniffs.

'It's not just the size,' I say. 'Although the size should be impossible too. There were other differences that didn't make sense.'

'Such as?' Hallie asks, using her sleeve to wipe the rain from her face.

'It's supposed to be a trapdoor spider, right? Everything we've seen so far has added up to that. But it has the eyes of a jumping spider.'

'Does it matter what kind of eyes it has?' Gus says.

'I think it might,' I say. 'Jumping spiders have big eyes because they use them to stalk and hunt. Trapdoor spiders sense vibrations from underground, so they don't need good eyesight. I think this spider can do both.'

'You think it can hunt above ground?' Naira says, turning pale like she was in the bug room.

'I mean, I don't know, but yeah, maybe. It's growing in confidence, venturing further out of its burrow. It stayed underground when it took Mr C, but we saw clear legs when it went for the chickens . . .'

'And just now it was almost fully out in the open.' Hallie nods.

'Well, this is unsettling news,' Gus says, as thunder rumbles again, further away this time.

'And another thing,' I say, because I might as well get it all out of the way in one go. 'When it jumped up between me and Klaus, it hesitated before it attacked, like it was thinking.'

'Spiders can't think,' Naira says.

'They don't usually think in that way, as far as I know,' I say. 'It ignored instinct and tried a new attack – like it learned from the last time.' I bite my lip, running through the facts and probabilities again in my mind, because I know it sounds crazy. 'I don't think it's just an oversized spider. I think it's been tweaked somehow.'

'Tweaked, as in someone has altered its DNA?' Naira says.

'It's the only explanation I can think of,' I shrug. 'I know you're afraid of them, but spiders are brilliant. They help the environment and hunt only to eat. They don't carry out revenge attacks or kill in cold blood.'

'You're saying someone has Jurassic-Worlded a spider?' Gus says. 'To make an evil super-spider?'

'I know it sounds nuts . . .' I say.

'But it actually totally makes sense,' Hallie nods. 'And I think we know who the Dr Wu is here. Or Dr Wus plural in this case.'

'Do we know if the Latchitts witnessed any of what just happened on the field?' I ask. 'There's no smoke coming from their chimney.'

'They left the cottage just after Gus drove off to rescue you on the lawnmower,' Naira says, and she and Hallie start laughing again. 'They walked across the paved area towards the sports hall, but I couldn't see them after that.'

'I wish I knew what they were planning on doing next,' I say.

'I've been thinking about them a lot.' Naira has given up with her dripping ponytail and is pulling her hair back in a tight braid.

'Ew,' Hallie says. 'I've been trying to do the opposite.'

'And I know you don't want to talk about it, but you asked how I ended up in detention, and I think it's relevant to this situation,' Naira

178

says. 'So I'm going to tell you what happened.'
She ties her braid with a hairband.

I start picking the skin around my fingernails
and keep my eyes fixed on my hands.

'So we're having this out?' Gus asks.
'You sure?'

Naira nods. 'If we're going to fix this disaster
of a situation, we need all the information we
can get. We're all here because of what
happened in the dining hall, but, for me at
least, there was more to that incident than
people saw.'

I glance up at that, surprised. I notice Gus
and Hallie react in a similar way to me, and
I start to think that maybe Naira is on to
something.

'So.' She takes a deep breath. 'I did
something a while back. Something I'm not
proud   of.
You know how much my mum is depending on
me to get into a top university so that
I can become a barrister and live a better life

than the one she's had, and all of that? She does everything for me. Works hard and spends every penny she has on my clothes and books, while she gets her stuff from car boots and charity shops.'

Her voice is getting louder and higher as she speaks. I can hear the panic in it – the pressure she feels.

'I can't let her down. I was desperate to get on the student council because it looks brilliant on your university application. It's the first step to eventually becoming Head Girl in the sixth form, and I need that – I really do. So after the votes were cast, I decided to check them – just to make sure I'd won. I was certain I'd have the most votes, but I didn't. I'd lost by three. So I removed five ballot papers. Destroyed them so that I'd win. I mean, it was despicable. Truly. But I told myself I wasn't hurting anyone, except the person who should have won.

'I didn't get caught, and as far as I knew,

nobody saw me do it or had any reason to think it had even happened.' Her cheeks have flushed pink again and seeing how hard it is for her to talk about this, I'm impressed by her courage. 'But a week ago I found an envelope in my locker. Inside was a note, and a photo.'

Hallie and Gus stare at her, but nobody says anything.

'The note was scrawled – handwriting I didn't recognise – and it said that the person who wrote it knew exactly what I'd done. The photo attached to it was of me with my hand in the ballot box – taken without me realising anyone was there. It was proof. The note said to make sure I was in the dining hall on Tuesday at twelve thirty, and to do something to get myself a Saturday consequence by the end of lunch, or the whole school would see what I did.'

I feel goosebumps rise on my arms. The rain is easing off again, but it's freezing on this roof, the wind blustering in angry gusts, making the clouds race across the sky. I feel cold to my bones. There's something going on here that is much bigger than we realised.

'So I spent the days I had left trying to track down the person who sent the note. I couldn't face people knowing the truth, but I also couldn't deal with the thought of getting a detention. I got nowhere, getting more and more frustrated and stressed each day. Then that lunchtime, when I saw the clock in the dining hall ticking towards one, I just panicked, and I lost it. Honestly, it was like an out-of-body experience. I heard myself screaming and watched myself pick up the tray of food and launch it across the room. It was like I had no power to stop it.' She looks at me. 'I didn't mean for it to hit you, Angelo. I'm sorry. It's my fault you're here.'

'It's not,' I say. 'I got a note in my locker too. With the same message. I did something that I'm ashamed of. Actually it's the worst thing that I ever did, because it hurt someone who didn't deserve it.' And as I'm saying it,

I realise that I've never fully admitted that to myself before. I'm no stranger to making mistakes or getting in trouble, but what I did earlier this term is the one thing I truly regret. 'The photo made me feel sick. But I'm not going to be blackmailed by anyone, so I ignored it, told myself I'd forgotten about it.'

I shove my hands in my pockets to stop myself from picking my skin any more. My fingers are starting to bleed.

'Then that lunchtime . . . I was starving. I knew there wasn't enough food at home for dinner for both me and my brother. I had enough money on my lunch card for chips, so I got them, knowing they'd be all I had to eat.' I pause. Take a breath. Not having enough money to eat is something I've never talked about to anybody. 'I was watching the clock as well, so I didn't see your lunch tray coming, Naira. When it hit me, I dropped my chips on the floor. I was gutted. But I was also just full of rage about the note and the photo and how awful I felt about what I did. So I lost it too. Flipped the table.'

'I'm so sorry about your food, Angelo.' Naira's eyes are filled with tears. Before today I hadn't seen her cry since Year 2.

'Honestly, it's fine,' I say. 'It was an accident. The table flip was on me.'

She leans forward and hugs me, and I don't think I've ever been more surprised by anything in my life, including that time when I saw a genetically mutated spider the size of a dog rise out of the earth.

'I got a note too,' Hallie says, when Naira lets me go. 'And yeah, I did something to a girl in our year that I hate myself for. I get loads of consequences anyway, so I felt like one more wouldn't really matter. I'd rather that than people see the photo. So I'd already come up with a bunch of stuff I could do to get a Saturday consequence that lunch. I prepared.'

'It was pretty impressive,' Gus says. 'Your one-woman protest.'

'I had the red paint in my bag. I thought if I'm going to deliberately do something to get in trouble, I might as well use it to make a point.'

'I barely noticed,' I say. 'I was too busy trying not to watch the clock. And failing.'

'I noticed,' says Gus. 'It was epic. She stood on the table and sprayed everyone around her with red paint, screaming "Meat Is Murder".'

Hallie shrugs. 'I didn't want to waste a consequence on something stupid.'

'You want to hear something weird?' Gus says.

We all look at him.

'I didn't get a note.'

I'm confused – it felt like we'd finally found a key to unlock some answers. Naira and Hallie look the same way I'm feeling.

'Just kidding.' Gus grins. 'I got a note and photo. You should have seen your faces.'

'Gus!' we all shout at the same time.

'So – long story short – I did a horrible thing too. I mentioned it earlier when we were in the biology classroom. There's something about me that I like to keep private, and the thing I did was to help cover it up. But I used someone else to do it, in a scummy way, and it was just really freaking nasty of me.'

I watch his face as he lets us into this secret part of himself. It's hard for him. He says it fast.

'So instead of being stressed about the blackmail, I thought I'd use it as an opportunity to do something I've always wanted to do.' He grins. 'Food fight.'

'We really caused chaos in the dining hall that day,' Hallie smiles.

I think we all feel better for sharing what we have. Guilt is like an endless weight, dragging you down, making every day hard. And although most of us have only told half our stories, it's enough for now. I wonder what Gus and Hallie did to make them feel so ashamed, but I let it go. We have something more important to focus on now.

CHAPTER FIFTEEN

'So I think we can guess who sent the notes,' Naira says.

'Mr Latchitt is everywhere around the school,' I say. 'You don't notice he's there half the time. He must have seen us doing the things we don't want to talk about.'

'And decided that we needed punishing,' says Hallie.

'Brutal punishment, though.' Gus pushes back his wet hair. 'Death by mutant spider is drastic, even for what I did. Any of you murder someone?'

We all shake our heads.

'So there's more to it than just our crimes,' Gus says. 'And why are the Latchitts messing with spider DNA anyway?'

'You're right,' I say. 'We need more information, and there's only one place we're going to find it.'

'You're going to tell me that you want to go to the gingerbread house, aren't you?' Gus sighs. 'You absolute madman.'

'Look, I don't know what the time is,' I say. Life without a phone in my pocket is at least a hundred times more confusing than normal. 'But at some point people are going to come looking for us. When they do, they're going to end up as spider food, unless we do something to stop them. We're here now, and we have a chance to find out what's going on. We might not get another one.'

'How do we know the spider hasn't already left the school grounds?' Hallie asks. 'It could be tearing up the high street as we speak.'

'I think it's being reined in by the train tracks and the main roads,' I say. 'The school boundaries all back on to places that are loud. Ground-dwelling spiders can feel the difference between a cricket, a bird, or whatever else might walk by, just by the vibrations. It probably knows better than to go near a train or a truck.'

'The Latchitts might have a working phone,' Naira says. 'And there could be evidence there that we can give to the police.'

'So we're really doing this?' Gus asks.

'We know they're out at the moment, creeping around,' I say, 'so if we're going, we should go now.'

Everyone groans. We're exhausted, wet and cold. My muscles ache, and my ankle feels bruised where the spider gripped me. Hallie must be in pain too, though obviously she doesn't say so. But we have a window of opportunity.

'This is all going to be over in a couple of hours,' I say. 'One way or another. We can rest then.'

'If we're alive,' Hallie says.

'How are we getting there?' Naira stands up and looks out across the field to the Latchitts'. 'I'm not excited about the prospect of running across the field again.'

'I can drive you all,' Gus says. 'But it will take a few trips. I don't think we can fit more than two of us at a time.'

'I get that it's the safest option, but it's so slow and loud. The Latchitts could hear it and come back. I say we just sprint across the field, all of us together in a tight group, so that the spider feels the vibrations and thinks we're something much bigger than we are. It might leave us alone. I really think we need to be fast.' I look round at the others as they weigh it all up.

Naira nods. 'Let's do it before I talk myself out of it.'

'It's all right for you two,' Gus groans. 'You're the fastest. I'll be the dude who gets picked off at the back.'

'We'll stay together – go fast but not flat

out,' I say. 'No one gets left behind.'

The rest of us stand and join Naira at the edge of the pigsty roof closest to the Latchitts'. It's maybe two hundred metres from here to their back gate.

'Four of us, one of him, right?' Hallie says. 'We got this.'

The roof is low enough that if we sit and dangle our legs over the edge, we can drop down on to the pig yard. So we sit.

'On three,' I say.

'Wait, *on* three, or . . .?' Gus asks.

'*On* three.' I scan the ground. The pigs are safe in their concrete-floored sty, but the rest of the pig yard is packed dirt and gravel.

'One . . .' I say, then a creak and a bang behind us makes us jump up and run to the other side of the roof. We look down to see that a sinkhole has opened up along one side of the building, and it's taken the mower. It's half in, half out, leaning at a dangerous angle like it could tip and fall completely at any second.

We stare at it in silence.

'Good thing we decided against driving,' Hallie says.

'Farewell, my beauty,' Gus says, raising his hand in a salute. 'You served us well and we will forever honour your name.'

'Was that an accident?' Naira asks as we head back over to our roof drop-off point. 'Or did the spider just – and I can't believe I'm even suggesting this – deliberately sabotage one of our only escape routes?'

We sit down again. 'I'd like to say it's not possible.' I grip the edge of the roof so I can balance right on the edge without falling. 'But after everything we've seen today, I honestly don't know. It's like the Latchitts have trained it to do what they want.'

'So now the Latchitts are both Dr Wu and Owen?' Gus says. 'Not fair – they get all the best parts.'

'The best part is obviously the velociraptor,' Hallie says.

'Yes!' Gus grins. 'And there are four of them, in a team. We can be the velociraptors.'

'Are you ready?' I say. 'Because we're going this time. One . . .'

'We need code names,' he says, and I appreciate that he's trying to distract either us or himself from the fear of heading back down.

'Two . . .'

'Angelo, you can be Alpha . . .'

'I want to be Alpha,' Hallie says. 'It shouldn't automatically go to a male.'

'Fine, Hallie is Alpha, Angelo is Romeo, Naira is Sierra . . .'

I snigger. 'Please say you're going to be Echo.'

'Why?' Gus asks.

'Because the initials spell a rude word,' Naira sighs. 'So juvenile.'

'That would be awesome.' Gus's face lights up. 'But I will inexplicably be called Red – the rogue of the team.'

'Right,' I say. 'Th—'

And with a crack and a rumble, the land

under our dangling feet suddenly falls away.

'Abort!' I shout, and we all scoot back as we watch the solid earth become a gash in the field, full of twisted fingers of broken roots and wriggling worms.

'Jesus.' I look down into the rift. It's only a couple of metres deep, but who knows how much further we could fall if the base of it gave way.

'That's two sides of the pigsty wiped out,' Hallie says. 'We're running out of ground to land on.'

A tremor to our left tells me another strip of earth has sunk.

'It's circling us like a shark,' Naira says. 'It's keeping us here.'

'We're safe here though, right?' Gus peers over the edge of the roof again. 'I mean, we could sit it out if we needed to?'

'I don't like the idea of being stuck here, exposed like this,' I say. 'If the Latchitts come back, we'd have nowhere to run. They could have weapons, or some other plan to hurt us –

we have no idea what they're thinking.'

'But we can't go down,' Gus says.

'Maybe we could go up.' I point at the oak tree that grows just behind the sty, some of its lower branches stretching over the roof we're sitting on. 'How are you at climbing trees?'

The oak is on the edge of the Dread Wood – a stretch of woodland that runs along the back of the field bordering the train tracks. It begins to the right of the pig yard and ends in the corner where the field meets the Latchitts' back fence.

'We could probably get to the Latchitts' without needing to touch the ground too often,' Hallie says. 'If we try to get from tree to tree, and use the shrubs and bushes.'

'The ground there is thick with roots,' I say. 'It's possible that the spider hasn't even burrowed there.'

'But it's trees,' Naira shudders. 'I hate trees. They're full of nature. And it's so wet and windy – it can't be safe.'

'Come on, Nai.' Gus puts an arm around her

and gives her a squeeze. 'We've taken on far worse things today than a few birds and caterpillars. And anyway, most of the trees are naked – we'll be able to see what's in them.'

'Either we all go, or none of us go,' I say. 'But I think it's our best chance.'

'Me too,' says Hallie.

'I'm in,' Gus says. 'Even though it sounds freaking awful.'

'OK,' Naira sighs. 'Let's do it. I assume you've climbed these trees before, Angelo?'

I grin at that. 'Maybe. I'll go first.'

The thickest branch that leans over the sty is basically flat, so it's a good starting point. I step on to it, as close to the trunk as I can where the branch is thickest, then it's just a jump to the centre where there are plenty of hand and footholds.

With the wind making the branches shake, the others wobble along behind me, and soon we're huddled amongst the bare twigs and ready to make our way through the Dread Wood.

CHAPTER SIXTEEN

HERD

The first ten minutes or so is easy enough. Well, the word easy has taken on a new meaning today. My shoulders ache from climbing and holding my weight as I hang from branches, and I'm scratched like an old phone screen. But nothing goes horribly wrong as we make our way deeper into the Dread Wood, using the branches to help keep our feet off the floor. Once we're in the thick of the trees, we're sheltered from the worst of the weather and we find thick, wiry bushes to use as stepping stones between them.

The ground looks undisturbed here, but we know better than to risk standing on it unless we absolutely have to.

A lot of the trees here are oak and ash, but there are others too, including some evergreens, which add a bit of colour amongst the shades of brown and grey. Finches sing around us from time to time, and though there aren't as many here as in the summer, it's a reassuring sound that makes me feel like being normal again is a possibility.

'So when we get to the house,' Gus says, crawling carefully along a wide branch – honestly, it's like he can't bear not to be talking – 'are we going to break in?'

'The door might be unlocked,' I say. 'It's not like they're expecting anyone to try to get in.'

'True,' Gus says. 'But what if they come back while we're inside?'

'We run,' I say.

'Or fight,' says Hallie. 'I'd love to take a swing at either of them. Maybe push her down the well. I've been thinking about it since the last time we were at their house.'

'Of course you have, Hal,' Gus says. 'I would expect nothing less.'

We're about halfway from the pigs to the Latchitts' fence, and deep in the middle of the Dread Wood. The sky growls – dark clouds chasing the clear patches of pale blue, spreading like smoke from a wildfire to make a low roof above us. The woodland around us noticeably darkens until it feels almost like we're enclosed in a bubble of grey.

'What's that thing called in English, where the weather reflects the sinisterness of the situation?' I ask.

'Pathetic fallacy,' Naira says.

The rest of us snort out a laugh.

'What?' Naira says.

'Just sounds rude,' Gus says. 'And Angelo, that's surprisingly poetic of you.'

'Angelo is quite poetic,' Naira says. 'He used to be brilliant at writing in primary.

He's smarter than people think he is.'

'So why don't you bother with schoolwork any more?' Gus asks.

'Can't see the point,' I say. 'I need to get a job as soon as I can, so it's not like I'll need the grades for university.'

'But if you have to be at school, which you do . . .' Hallie steps on to a tree stump and looks across at me, 'you might as well make a bit of an effort. You never know what could happen in the future.'

'You could go to uni and study zoology,' Naira says. 'Or natural history, then spend your life travelling the world.'

'Can't leave my brother,' I say, joining Hallie on the stump, which is just about wide enough for the two of us.

'Your brother will be able to look after himself one day, though,' says Gus.

Naira jumps on to a fallen log, just a metre ahead of us. Hallie and I are on the stump, and Gus is perched in a tree, just behind and to our right. We're entering a small clearing – maybe six metres wide and eight metres long. I look up at the clear view of the churning clouds, as a fat drop of rain splashes down on to my hair. The birds have stopped singing and the air is thick with the smell of rotting leaves. A movement catches my eye, in the tree above Gus. It's not much, just a slight rustle that makes a couple of pine needles fall to the ground, but it's enough to get my attention.

'Gus,' I say. 'Drop down on to the stump. We'll make room.'

'Why?' he asks, looking over his shoulder into the pine trees.

There's another swish in the branches over his head. Needles drop on to his upturned face.

'You all saw that, right?' he says.

'The stump,' I say as Hallie darts forward on to Naira's log so that Gus can drop down.

But Gus is transfixed, staring up through the branches. 'There's something up there.'

'Please tell me that vile spider hasn't

climbed up a tree.' Naira is staring upwards too. 'It was supposed to stay in the ground.'

'But the eyes,' I say. 'They're like a jumping spider's. I don't know why it would have those, unless . . .'

'Oh shiz,' Gus says, turning himself around on the branch so that he can make the jump to the stump. 'Oh shizzing, shizzery shiz.'

'Wait, what was that?' Naira spins around, almost losing her balance on the log. She's looking into the trees on the other side of the clearing. 'I swear I saw something.'

'Gus, you need to jump,' I say as the narrower branches above him start to part, and the tips of two big, brown legs appear. 'Right now.'

Gus jumps, just as the spider launches itself towards him. It lands on the branch where he was just sitting, then disappears back into the tree. I grab Gus as he topples backwards, almost falling off the stump. He's shaking.

'That's twice today,' he gasps as I steady

him. 'I'm gonna need to start staying upright, or I'll end up having a comedy death that will turn into a viral social media phenomenon.'

I put my hand on his shoulder and smile. 'Just think of the memes.'

He grins back.

'We need to get moving,' I say.

'But where?' Naira says, still staring into the trees. 'The ground's not safe. The trees aren't safe . . .'

'Away from the evergreens,' I say. 'The spider won't have camouflage and we'll see it coming. Straight ahead, across the clearing, then a few more metres and we're clear.'

'Guys,' Hallie says. 'Naira's right, there's definitely something in that tree over there.'

I look towards where she's pointing. Ahead of us, at the other end of the clearing, there's a big, old yew tree. Its trunk is twisted and lined, dividing close to the ground into gnarled, ivy-covered branches. It's thick with needles that shiver in the wind. As I watch, there's a moment of stillness, and then a strong gust bends every tree around us, making them creak and groan. Something stirs on the trunk of the yew.

A crackle just behind and to the left of me makes me spin around, my heart lurching in my chest, to peer into the depths of a shed-sized holly shrub. Between the shiny green leaves and red berries, there is something else gleaming in the weak shafts of sunlight that make it through the foliage. It's ink black, and although I can't see it clearly, I can make out enough of it to know it's big, and it's alive.

'There's more than one,' I whisper, certainty hitting me like a gut punch as I say it. Then I shout, 'There's more than one. We need to move.' But there's no time.

A spider – wolf grey and the size of a bulldog – leaps out of the yew tree and into the clearing, blocking us from moving in the direction we were headed. It raises its head, showing downward-curling fangs, dripping with venom. Naira screams. A glossy black spider shoots out of the holly, and lands lightly in the space to the left of us. This one has thinner legs, but its abdomen is horribly large and bulbous, and has a skull-shaped red marking that looks about as menacing as you'd think. And then there's our old friend Big Brown crawling down the tree behind us.

'They're pack-hunting us,' Gus shouts. '*They* are the freaking velociraptors.'

'What do we do?' Naira whispers.

We're surrounded. Wolf Grey takes a couple of steps towards us. We need to stay away from those fangs. I look around for a weapon, and luckily the strong winds have given me plenty of options. I grab a thick piece of fallen branch from the ground and grip it like a baseball bat.

'Get behind me,' I shout.

'Stuff that,' Hallie says, and I glance across to see that she's grabbed a branch too. 'Not letting you get all the action.'

'Ooh, a pointy one.' Gus holds the stick he's picked up like a spear.

Naira steps off the log, her eyes not leaving Wolf Grey, and feels around for a branch of her own. 'We all fight.'

Hallie steps down next to her, and Gus and I move slowly towards them, me keeping eyes on Red Skull, and Gus watching Big Brown. We join up, standing back-to-back.

'They move, we swing,' Hallie says. 'Got it?' She's the opposite side of our huddle, so I can't see her, but I picture her fierce expression, and I'm glad I have her covering my back.

'Hal thinks she's Harley Quinn,' Gus says.

Naira rolls her shoulders. 'This is just like playing softball, right?'

'Exactly,' I say. 'Anything flies towards you, you swing at it as hard as you can.'

'Shouldn't we stand a bit less close to each other?' Gus says. 'Much as I'm fond of you guys, I don't want to take a branch to the head.'

'He's right,' Naira says. 'Two paces out on . . .'

'Not on three, please,' Hallie says. 'That never works out well.'

'OK, on "go" then,' Naira says.

'We stay back-to-back and try to keep moving forward if we can,' I say. I adjust the grip on my branch bat.

'Who moves first? Us or them? I don't know what the rules are.' Gus is bouncing on his toes.

'The great thing about this situation, Gus,' says Hallie, 'is that there are no rules. We can do anything. I suggest you take every bit of anger you've ever kept locked up inside, and channel it into kicking spider ass.'

'OK, two paces apart on "go", and then we start edging across the clearing,' Naira says. 'Ready . . .'

I take a deep breath in through my nose. Try to calm my racing heart.

'Steady . . .'

Red Skull taps her front right leg into the leaf litter like she's impatient to get started, then

she rears up, lifting her front two legs above
her head, and hissing. I don't dare take my
eyes off her for even half a second. I try not to
blink.

'Go!'

CHAPTER SEVENTEEN

TACTICS

I take two steps forward, feeling instantly a stark coldness where the heat of the others just was. I don't usually like being close to people, but this is definitely an exception.

Red Skull waves her front legs in the air, making herself as tall and wide as possible. The tips of her toes reach as high as my waist, so it's an alarming sight. Her fangs are wide at the base, and taper into vicious points that hook inwards. If she gets those fangs into me, she's not letting go. I swing my branch a couple of times, not trying to hit anything, just as a warning. I mean,

209

given what we've learned today, the chances of her backing down and deciding not to attack are slim. But it's worth a try.

She scuttles back a couple of steps, her legs moving with speed and confidence. She's not really afraid of me, she's just assessing if I pose any threat at all, and the best way to take me down. I'm desperate to see how the others are getting on but I know I can't take my eyes off Red Skull.

'We good?' I shout.

'Peachy,' Hallie shouts back.

'Gus?' I say.

'Define good.'

'Nai?'

'Meh.'

'So let's start moving forward. We need to get out of here.' I take a sidestep in the right direction.

Red Skull crouches, and then springs upwards with impressive speed. I don't stop to look, or think, I just swing. As hard as I can. My bat connects with her abdomen and she's knocked off course and into a tree trunk. She instantly rights herself and turns to face me again. I feel a stab of fear. I thought it would be like hitting a large baseball, but it's more like trying to bat away a boulder flying towards you. She's heavy and strong, and my hit did no damage to her at all. I don't think we can beat the spiders this way.

'Duck!' Gus shouts, and I dip my head just in time to see Big Brown zipping above me. Gus must have made enough contact to bat him away but not enough to take him down. Big Brown lands close to Red Skull and scrambles to get up. His back legs are injured, and he's trying to move without putting too much weight on them. It must have been from when Gus ran over his burrow lid on the field and trapped his feet.

'That's mower power,' Gus says next to me, and I can hear the grin in his voice.

The two spiders dart towards us, close enough to be threatening but out of reach of our weapons. They scuttle about, randomly and unpredictably jumping at us, then backing off. Gus and I stay close, manoeuvring ourselves so that we keep them in our sights.

'What are they doing?' Gus asks. 'Why don't they attack us properly? You think they're scared?'

'No, I don't,' I say. 'It's like they're planning something.'

I hear a roar of rage. It sounds like Hallie, but it can't be because it's coming from too far away – right across the other side of the clearing.

'Watch them for a sec,' I say to Gus. 'Shout if they get close.'

'Affirmative.'

With Gus on guard, I risk a glance over my shoulder to see where Hallie and Naira are. I swear out loud when I see they are much further away than I expected – right on the treeline diagonally opposite from where we are. Naira is using her branch to stab at Wolf Grey from one side, while Hallie swings at it from another. It's a good technique, but Wolf is fast and avoids all of their attempts, at the same time creeping and jumping so that they're heading into the trees.

'They're trying to separate us,' I gasp. 'We're weaker apart.'

'Great,' Gus says, jabbing his spear at Big Brown. 'We're being outsmarted by creatures whose knees are higher than their faces.'

'Guys!' I shout. 'We need to huddle. Make for that small blackthorn.'

'What the hell is a small blackthorn?' Naira shouts back. I'm not sure Hallie's even heard me – she's so focused on caving the spider's head in.

'Twiggy bush, three metres to your right,' I yell. Then I turn back to Big Brown and Red Skull, balance my branch to my left hand for a moment, so I can flex the fingers on my right, then I grip it again and give it a swing. 'Gus, we're going to move forward swinging so that they fall back a bit, and then we're going to shift to the blackthorn to meet the girls.'

'Got it,' Gus says, and we both power forward, driving the spiders back into the trees, and then we half backwards, half sideways run towards the bush.

'Hallie, now!' Naira shouts, and they do the same to Wolf Grey, Hallie managing to give it a glancing blow to the face.

'Yes!' she whoops as they retreat to the blackthorn.

'Hey,' Naira says, when they reach us. 'What's up?'

'I think they're trying to separate us so they can take us down one at a time,' I say. I'm out of breath. We all are. It's good to feel the others at my back again, and I feel like I have enough left in me to make one last play.

'We need to stay together,' I say. 'They don't like taking us on as a pack.'

'I think we should focus on getting out of the Dread Wood,' Naira says. 'We have a better chance running across the field than we do with them dropping out of the trees on to our heads.'

'Agreed,' I say.

'Easy for you two to say,' Gus huffs. 'You're like human cheetahs.'

'We'll stay together,' I say again. 'We'll run as fast as we can without anyone getting left behind.'

'I'd rather stay here and smush some spider,' Hallie says, expertly twirling her branch like you see people do in the movies.

'We can't win like this,' I say. 'They're too fast. Come on, Hal, I know you prefer to fight than to run, but there's no point throwing your life away on a battle you're going to lose.'

She doesn't answer straight away. I watch the spiders circling, getting closer. Wolf Grey in front, Big Brown to the right, and Red Skull to the left.

'OK,' she says finally. 'What's the best way out?'

'Past Wolf Grey,' I say, eyeing the biggest of the spiders. She's a beast, covered in hairs as thick as pencils.

'Aw, you've named her!' Gus says. 'That's so cute.'

'But how do we get past her?' Naira says. 'Any ideas?'

'Easy,' Gus says. 'Roman wedge formation. We learned about it in Year 4 at primary. One of us takes the point and heads straight at her.'

'I want to be the point,' Hallie says.

'Two of us go each side of the point and slightly behind to form a "V" shape, sweeping the left and right to push the enemies outwards,' Gus carries on. 'Then one person goes back-to-back with the point, facing the rear to protect our asses. If we make it past Wolf we reverse the wedge. Simple.'

'Wait, go through that again,' Hallie says.

'Hallie, you go in front, face the way we're heading and charge at Wolf Grey swinging like you mean it,' Gus says. 'Angelo, stand just behind Hallie and to the right, Naira, just behind and to the left. You three face forward and swing with everything you've got – we need a massive show of aggression. Swing at different levels – high, medium height, and low, to keep the enemy guessing. I'll take the rear, with my pointy stick poking upwards to protect us from overhead adversaries, and another one pointing behind to jab outwards.' He picks up a snapped-off branch with a sharp end. 'This will work great. As soon as we pass Wolf and the spiders are behind us, we change position, so Hallie steps forward to be level with Nai and Ang – can I call you Ang? – so you're side by side. Then I'll be at the front with Mister Pointy Stick, and his best friend, Lady Pointy Stick. We swing, jab and keep moving until we've left the woods. Got it?'

'Should have asked you right at the start,' I say.

'Yeah, Gus, check you out with the knowledge.' Hallie swings at Red Skull who is creeping forward.

'And to think we were following Angelo's rubbish plan,' Naira snorts, and we all laugh.

'Let's do it,' I say. 'Everyone ready?'

'Yep.' Naira.

'Yeah.' Gus.

'More than ready,' Hallie says. 'I am pumped.'

'Are we doing a countdown, or a "ready, steady go"?' Gus says.

'Neither,' I say. 'Let's just go now.'

We start moving towards the spiders with as much energy and confidence as we can, swinging aggressively at different heights and angles, just like Gus said.

'Come on, you ugly scum dogs,' Hallie shouts. 'Let me mash up your ooky . . .' she swings, 'skeazy . . .' she swings again, 'nasty buggy faces.'

I try to match her ferocity, though I'm not sure that's even possible. Red Skull hesitates for a moment and then jumps to the side. I swing at her and feel my branch make contact – one of the sharp twig stubs coming out of the end piercing one of her eyes. She shrieks and falls back. Big Brown retreats too.

He's less confident than the others because of his injured legs I think. That leaves Wolf Grey who, so far, is standing her ground.

'I'm gonna go for it,' Hallie says. I wonder what 'going for it' looks like if that's not what she's been doing already. Then she charges forward, literally roaring, whirling her branch like a samurai sword. She's terrifying. If she was coming at me like that, I'd be halfway across the field by now, running for my life. But Wolf takes just a step or two back and rubs its legs on the area around its face which creates a sound like nothing I've ever heard – like something between a bark, and a . . .

'Is it farting out of its face?' Naira squeaks.

'It's warning us off,' I say.

'I've done farts louder than that in my sleep,' Hallie shouts, swiping at the spider's neck with her branch.

Wolf Grey clacks her pincers at us, crouches, and then launches herself into the air. Her legs are splayed as she flies towards our faces.

'I got this!' Gus shouts as he thrusts his upright pointy stick towards Wolf. It scrapes her abdomen and she twists in the air, going off course and landing heavily behind us.

'Reverse the wedge!' Gus shouts, and we change position so that Hallie, Naira and I are facing the spiders in the clearing. Wolf has landed clumsily, and is picking herself up. Red Skull and Big Brown have backed away.

'We did it,' shouts Hallie. 'They know they're beaten. Have that, you manky dump stains.'

Wolf turns, pointing her wounded abdomen at us.

'Is she going to fart out of her butt this time?' Hallie says.

She rubs her legs against her body again. I expect another weird noise. I don't expect the spiny hairs from her body to come shooting towards us like missiles.

CHAPTER EIGHTEEN

GINGERBREAD HOUSE

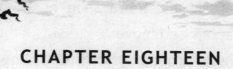

There's an instant explosion of pain as one of the hairs strikes me in the chest, and another in my face. I cry out, at the same time as Hallie, Gus and Naira do. We've all taken hits. The hairs have pierced my skin. The one in my face falls out when I shout, but the one in my chest is embedded and stays put, sticking out of me like a hedgehog spine. I can't stop to take it out – not when we're so close to getting out of the Dread Wood.

'Keep focused,' Naira shouts. 'Hold on to your weapons and move.'

And we do, carefully at first while we keep an eye on the spiders, and then faster as they fall behind, looking like they want to regroup as much as we do.

'Almost there,' Gus shouts as we crash through the trees, trying to stay alert and not allow the excitement of being so close distract us from the threat of the spiders, who could have climbed back into the trees and be moving in for another attack.

And then we're out, on to the field, close to the Latchitts' fence. We run, keeping together, heading for the back entrance to the Latchitts' yard. Every instinct I have wants me to pull out the hair that's protruding from my chest – it looks all kinds of wrong – but I know we can't stop until we get somewhere spider-free. Right now, awful as it is, the closest safe place is the Latchitts' cottage.

I open their back gate a crack and peer through.

'Garden is clear,' I say.

We move in, still clutching our weapons, and creep to the house. There's no smoke coming from the chimney and when we look through the windows, there are no lights switched on inside. Everything is quiet and still.

'It could be a trap,' Naira says, craning her neck to get a view into as many nooks as possible. She has two spider hairs sticking out of her shoulder.

'Yeah,' Hallie says. 'But we don't have much choice. We need answers. And besides, there's nowhere else to go without running across the field again.'

I turn the handle of the back door and pull. It opens with a creak.

'Why would they leave it open?' Gus whispers. 'It's like they want us to come in.'

'Maybe they do,' I say. 'Since Mr Canton went under, they've not tried to hide what they're up to. If anything, they've been putting on a show for us, like they want us to see.'

'But why?' Hallie says. 'It's like they hate us.'

'Yeah, it is,' I say. 'There must be a reason.'

'And it's like they're not scared of getting in trouble,' Gus says. 'Either they don't care if they go to prison . . .'

'. . . or they don't think they're going to get caught.' I bite my lip and look into the house – dim and silent and waiting. For us. I'm scared, I realise. The most scared I've been all day. 'Going in is a risk,' I say.

We look at each other, and I can see from their pale faces and wild, tired eyes that they're all just as scared as I am.

'If we don't go in and get some answers,' Hallie says, 'we're going to regret it for the rest of our lives. I don't know about you guys, but I really need to understand what's going on here. I'm going in. I'll go alone if you want, and you can wait here and keep a lookout.'

'If you're going in, I am too,' I say. 'We do better when we stick together.'

'Me too,' Gus says.

'We check the house first, and if they're not here we find somewhere to sit and take these goddamn spikes out. Then we snoop,' Naira says.

And that's it. Decision made.

We make our way through the house, room by room, keeping our weapons ready and covering each other's backs. The kitchen, living room and office room downstairs are empty of people. They're not lurking in the cupboard under the stairs, but we do find a duffel bag packed with clothes, and a suitcase half filled with books and ornaments, and half empty. It's been left open, like they're planning to come back and fill it in the not too distant future.

'Looks like they're planning on leaving soon,' Naira says. 'That can't be a good sign.'

We head upstairs.

'I feel like a SWAT officer, but more rustic,' Gus says, wiggling his stick. 'Bathroom clear.'

'The small bedroom is clear too,' Hallie says.

'Just the main bedroom left.' I nod towards

the master bedroom. The door is slightly open and I can see the Latchitts' perfectly made bed. 'Hal, do you want to check in the wardrobe, and I'll look under the bed?'

'Sure,' she says. 'Although I so don't want to see what they have in their wardrobe.'

'It could be worse,' Gus shudders. 'At least we don't need to feel around in their drawers.'

'Let's get this over with,' I say, and I spring into the room, fall into a crouch and look under the bed to find nothing but a couple of pairs of slippers and a friendly house spider. I give it a smile and leave it to its dusty corner.

'Nothing of interest in here,' Hallie calls. 'I think we're safe to rest for a minute if we stay by the windows to keep a lookout.'

'Thank god,' Gus says, backing up down the hall so we can all go downstairs ahead of him.

We move into the living room, and pull the sofa over to the window so we can watch while we talk.

'Let's sort these spikes out,' I say. I can feel

blood running down my face. 'Let me check where this one fell out before we remove the rest. Just in case.'

There's a mirror on one of the walls that I use to inspect the wound left by the hair. There's a small puncture, which is bleeding a bit but not enough to need a stitch. The hole is perfectly round, no ragged edges or any sign of anything left behind that might need digging out. The skin around it is turning angry red, and it's starting to itch and burn.

'I think we're good to take them out,' I say, pulling at the one in my chest. 'But go carefully – try not to snap the spines as you remove them.'

Hallie has three in her forearm, which come out easily but she bleeds a lot. One of Naira's starts to break as she pulls it, so it takes a bit of time to get it free.

'Didn't you get hit, Gus?' Hallie asks as she wraps a bandage we found in a first-aid kit around her arm.

'I did, and I might need help getting it out 'cos I can't see it properly,' he sighs, turning around to show us his behind. 'Just my luck to take one in the butt.'

I bite my lip, and there's a moment of strained silence where I think we're all really, really trying to keep it together. But then we all splutter into laughter, including Gus, whose butt spine wobbles around as he does. Eventually, we stop, and Naira gently pulls the hair out for Gus, who looks like he wants to crawl into a hole and die.

'I'll put the plaster on myself,' he says, grabbing a bunch from the first-aid kit, and hobbling into the hallway. He's out of sight, but he's left the door open so he can hear.

'My arm is on fire,' Hallie says, flapping it around and blowing on it, even though it's not going to make a bit of difference. 'Why does it hurt so much?'

'There's an irritant on the hairs,' I say. 'Some species of tarantula have it, I think. It shouldn't do any lasting damage but it can itch and hurt like a son of a beast.'

'Spiders really are the gift that keeps on giving,' Naira says, wincing. 'Are you sure it's not like the venom?'

'I don't think so.' I shake my head. 'The venom from a normal spider's fangs is different to the stuff on their hair. We'd be paralysed by now if it was the same.'

'I guess at least none of us got one in the eye.' Gus walks back in and attempts to sit himself down on the sofa. 'So what next?'

We drink water from the taps, but though all of us are hungry, we don't want to risk eating any of the Latchitts' food, in case they've sabotaged it. And although we saw most of the house when we were checking the Latchitts weren't there, we decide it's worth a closer look to make sure there's nothing we've missed. This is probably the only opportunity we'll have to learn more about the odd couple and what they're up to.

We take it in turns to keep watch while the others search the rooms, opening drawers and cupboards, and feeling behind items on shelves to see if there's anything hiding that might help us.

Hal and I decide to check the downstairs office. Well, I'm calling it an office, but it's more of a muddled room that looks like it's used for a load of different things. As we walk in the door, there's a small table with a large object on top, covered in a cloth.

'What do you think is under there?' Hallie whispers.

I shrug. 'Severed heads?'

Hallie slowly moves her hand towards the cloth and takes hold of a corner. A shrill whistle from whatever's underneath makes her jerk backwards, the cloth still in her hand so it slides off the object in one quick movement.

'Thank god,' Hallie says, when we see that standing on the table is a birdcage containing two small finches. They seem unharmed, and they hop from perch to perch.

'Why is their water red?' Hallie asks, peering at the upside-down bottle attached to the cage. It's made of glass, and half filled with red liquid. It has a thin silver tube that reaches in through the bars so that the birds can drink from it, and as I watch, a single red droplet falls from the end, splashing down on to the floor of the cage. One of the finches whistles again – a couple of notes this time – and I recognise it as the start of 'Incy Wincy Spider'. It sings it again and again, but it can't get past the first part.

'He's teaching the birds to whistle his song.' Hallie bends down to pick up the cloth from where she dropped it on the floor. 'Super creepy. Let's cover them back up.'

I help her cover the cage again, and the finches fall quiet.

There's an old wooden desk with a shelving bit attached to it with a bunch of cubbyholes and tiny drawers. Sitting on top of it is an old shoebox, which of course I open. Inside there are photographs and articles cut out of newspapers.

'Old people are so weird keeping stuff like that when you can just save it on your phone,' Hallie snorts.

'Look, though,' I say, picking one of the paper clippings up. It's dated fifteen years ago, and is an article about scientific advances in the field of DNA research. There's a photo of two scientists working in a lab – a hulk of a man, and a tiny lady beside him.

'It's the Latchitts!' Hallie squeaks. 'Although under the photo it says they are "Dr Lachey and Dr Lachey: the husband and wife team at the forefront of research in this country."'

'They must have changed their names,' I say.

'They changed their whole lives,' says Hallie. 'How did they go from being important scientists to school groundskeepers? Something's happened somewhere along the way.'

I flick through the rest of the stuff in the box. There are photos of the Latchitts when they were younger, smiling together, with Mrs Latchitt holding a baby. Then others of them on the beach, and at the park with a little girl.

'They must have a daughter,' I say. 'They look like normal people in these.'

'I wonder where she is.' Hallie picks up a picture of the girl smiling in front of a Christmas tree with a doll in her arms. 'I can't see any pictures of her as an adult, and she must be grown up by now. Just look at the eighties vibe in that living room.'

There's nothing else of interest in the box, and we're aware that we don't have much time, so we close it and move on.

There are two armchairs, worn and faded, facing each other over a small circular coffee table.

'Nice coasters,' Hallie says, picking up a square pad from the coffee table. It has a picture of a sunset and says 'Blessed are those who light the way for others'. The other one shows a path winding through a forest, and the words 'Faithless is he that says farewell when the road darkens – J.R.R. Tolkien'.

'I never get why people have these,' I say.

'Coasters?' Hallie looks up. 'Really?'

I shrug.

'They're for putting your mugs on so you don't leave marks on the furniture.' She puts the sunset one down. 'What do you use in your house?'

'The table,' I say. 'Or the floor, the arm of the chair, the windowsill. Whatever, really.'

We move across the room to the window, which looks out on to the backyard. It's raining again, drops spattering the glass and thunking down on the roof above us. On our right, behind the door, there's an unusual-looking cupboard attached to the wall. It has two rectangular wooden doors covering a frame that's about a metre wide and eighty centimetres tall, but only about five centimetres deep. The doors are scratched and dented, but more through being old and used a lot than any deliberate damage. I pull them open, expecting to see another nature picture with an inspirational quote written over it. What I find makes my mouth fall open and my breath catch in my throat.

'What the actual hell?' Hallie says, standing next to me and staring at the wall.

My eyes rove over what's in front of us, my brain struggling to catch up and compute what I'm seeing. 'We should get the others.'

CHAPTER NINETEEN

NO SECRETS

There's a corkboard behind the doors. It's light and lifts out easily, so we take it into the living room where we can all look over it while still watching the front of the house.

'Guys,' Hallie says. 'You need to see this.'

I lean the board against the back of the sofa, face out, so that we can all get a good view.

It's not easy to look at. I find myself veering between anger, humiliation and shock, as I try to take in what I'm seeing. Nobody says anything, so I reckon they're all going through the same thing.

It's a corkboard – the kind you can pin things on to, like reminders and lists and memories. It's covered, corner-to-corner, in photos. Of us.

Of course the pictures I look at first are the ones of me. They've been taken over the past few months – since not long after I started at Dread Wood High, right up until this week. There's one of me flipping the table in the dining hall. They show every bad thing I've done since I've been here: flipping the finger to Mr Cox in maths; shoving Harley Mills because he got in my face; ripping pages out of my French book to make paper planes. There are loads of me sitting alone, on the backs of benches; leaning up against the tennis court fence; on the science block roof. And in the middle of them all is the photo that was sent with the blackmail note.

'I need to tell you what I did,' I say. 'The reason I'm here. You're going to see the picture now anyway. It must be important – part of the reason why we're here.'

I put my finger on the photo. I burned my copy straight away, but it's like the image burned into my brain at the same time. I've thought about it at least twenty times a day since. It shows me with my hand in someone's bag, pulling something out. It's clearly not my bag, and the look on my face shows that I shouldn't be doing what I'm doing. I look shady as hell.

'Go for it,' Naira says. 'It can't be worse than what I did.'

I take a breath. 'OK, so, I came to Dread Wood High set on keeping myself to myself. I was going to be coming in as little as possible, just enough to keep the school off my parents' backs, and my parents off my back. But a couple of weeks into being here, this girl I sat next to in English started talking to me. She was nerdy as hell, but smart and funny.' I pause. Rub at the puncture mark on my face.

'She made me laugh, and I realised I liked hanging out with her. So without meaning to, I'd sort of made a friend.' I expect one of the others to make a joke, but they don't. They're listening.

'Then, about a month ago, I was having a bad week. I hadn't even seen my parents for a couple of days, because they were working. It was nearly the end of the month and there was no food left in the house. I knew when I collected my brother from the neighbour's after school that there wouldn't be anything to give him for dinner. So, long story short, I went into her bag to steal some money. She saw me and she was so hurt. She wanted to know why I'd done it. I was ashamed, and angry at the world, I guess, and I didn't want her to feel sorry for me, so I shouted a load of abuse at her and stormed off. Haven't spoken to her since.'

I look up at the others for the first time since I started talking. I don't know what I expect to see on their faces – disgust, or ridicule maybe. But I don't see any.

'It's the worst thing I've done in my life. Well, the thing I feel the most guilty about anyway. I wish I could take it back.'

'Thanks for telling us,' Hallie says. 'And as a way of making you feel better, let me tell you what my photo's all about.' She flicks a picture on the board. It's Hallie, stuffing what looks like artwork in a bin. 'So I was leading a debate in ethics class about the death penalty. Obviously I was arguing against it – it's barbaric and I can't believe that it's still happening in loads of countries, even now. Anyway, the girl who was told to argue for it had really done her homework. Her points were clever, and she had found statistics to back them up. And she was just so damn articulate. I got angrier and angrier until I was fuming so hard, I just started screaming abuse at her.'

So far, so Hallie.

'I got after-school detention, obviously,

and it was being run by Miss Grogan, so it was in the art block. While I was there, I saw this girl's art project drying on one of the racks, and when the teacher left the room for a minute, I took it and stuffed it in my bag.

I sat through the rest of the detention thinking about it screwed up at the bottom of my backpack. I mean, I knew it was ruined because the paint was wet and I'd smeared it everywhere.' She stops and chews on the inside of her mouth for a bit. I can see how hard this is for her. 'So when we left, I stuffed it into one of the bins outside the classroom block and covered it with a load of rubbish. The girl failed her art assessment because she had nothing to hand in. I mean, I shout, and I fight, and I lose my temper, but I don't usually sneak around and do snaky stuff behind people's backs. That's not me, or at least I didn't think it was. And that poor girl didn't even agree with the death penalty anyway, she was just doing the assignment because she was told to. I heard her crying in the toilet. I've honestly never felt so ashamed.'

Tears start rolling down her face, and she wipes her nose with her bad arm, wincing at the pain, and then wiping again even harder.

I wrap my arm around her shoulder and give her a squeeze. I'm not going to say what she did wasn't bad, and I don't think she wants to hear that anyway. But I understand how she feels, and maybe that's enough.

'OK, my turn, before I lose my balls,' Gus says. 'I've half told you anyway, but the full story includes something really personal. Something I haven't told anyone at this school.'

'Nothing any of us say is going to leave this gingerbread house, right?' I look at the others. 'I know I'm not going to tell anyone anything.'

'No offence, man, but you don't have any mates so you've got no one to tell,' Gus says, making us all laugh.

'Everything here is between us,' Hallie says.

'Definitely.' Naira nods.

Gus blows out a breath. Swallows. 'To tell this tale,' he says in a granny voice, 'I have to start way back, a long, long time ago, in a land far away, where a beautiful baby boy was born. His parents named him Gustav, and everyone agreed he was the best child that ever existed. Then one day . . .' his voice turns normal again, 'when he was three years old, he got sick. Turned out he had a serious illness that meant his digestive system didn't work properly. He had lots of tests and spent a few years in and out of hospital. He missed loads of school, which sounds awesome, but was actually horrible, and eventually, when he was in Year 1, he needed an operation to save his life.'

I don't know what I was expecting, but it wasn't this. I can't think of anything to say.

'The operation worked – hooray – but it meant that little Gustav would have a . . .' he pauses and wrinkles his nose like he's thinking of the best way to say it, 'thing to deal with for the rest of his life.' He pauses again. 'Sod it, I'm just going to show you. Are you ready for the big reveal, guys?'

I honestly have no idea what he's going to show us.

He lifts his sweatshirt and untucks his polo top, raising it enough to show his stomach area. On the left side of his stomach, below his belly button there's a flattish plastic pouch, about the size of a book, fitted close to his skin. I have never seen anything like it in my life, and I have no idea what it is. Looking at Naira and Hallie's faces, I'd say they're feeling the same way I am.

'I had my large intestine removed,' Gus says. 'I can't poo like a normal person, so the surgeons made a stoma, which is like a little tube opening out through a hole, here . . .' He points to the middle of the bag. 'The pouch is fitted over it to collect my waste because I can't dump it into the toilet like the rest of you. So yeah, I carry my turd around in a bag.' He pokes a photo on the board, which is of him disappearing into a disabled toilet. 'You have to change it a lot. Sometimes it leaks, so you're like constantly paranoid. It leaked in biology once, and it stunk like you wouldn't believe. I blamed the girl I was sitting next to, and everyone started laughing at her. Then I joined in with everyone for days while they made up names for her and generally made her life miserable. I could see she was getting upset, but I didn't want anyone to know it was me, so I carried on. It was horrible. *I* was horrible.'

'Jesus,' I say. 'I had no idea.'

'And that's the way I like it,' Gus says. 'I know most people would be cool with it, but some would think I'm disgusting. And I'll literally never get a girlfriend if it gets out.'

'I'd be your girlfriend, Gus,' Naira says. Then turns bright pink. 'I mean, your pouch wouldn't put me off at all if I wanted to be your girlfriend.'

'Same,' says Hallie. 'Everyone has stuff they're embarrassed of, and this is honestly no big deal.

I mean, it's a big deal in what you went through and what you have to manage every day, but it would never make me think less of you.'

'Agreed,' I say. 'I'd still snog you.' And I lean over and plant a big kiss on his cheek. I think it surprises me as much as it does everyone else, because we all start laughing, and don't stop for a good few minutes.

'Thanks, guys,' Gus says, when we finally calm down. 'It's so beautiful to share this moment with you, here, in the house of two psychopaths as we face certain doom.'

'You already know what I did,' Naira says, pointing at a photograph showing her with her hand inside the ballot box. 'I'm disgusted with myself.'

'Naira, you've literally never broken a rule in your life,' says Hallie. 'You made one mistake. You're standing with three people who have made loads – no offence, guys.'

'None taken,' I say.

'You speak only the truth,' says Gus.

'The fact that you feel so bad about it says a lot,' I say.

'Same for all of you.' Naira still looks sad but manages a half-smile.

'Out of interest, who should have won if you hadn't changed the votes?' Hallie asks.

'Colette Huxley,' says Naira.

It's like being woken up by your phone alarm when you've left the volume on full and fallen asleep with it next to your ear.

'Colette Huxley,' I repeat.

'Do you know her?' Naira asks. 'She's in Seven S, I think, but I've not seen her in school for a few weeks.'

'I know her,' I say. 'I stole money out of her bag.' I nod at the photo of me doing it.

Naira's mouth falls open.

'I destroyed her art project,' Hallie says.

'Yeah,' Gus says. 'I blamed her for my rancid stink.'

'Colette Huxley,' I say again. I've not even let myself think her name for weeks, because it made me feel so ashamed. 'Guys, I think we've found our link.'

'What does Colette Huxley have to do with any of this?' Naira says. 'And how is she connected to the Latchitts?'

'Has anyone even seen her lately?' Hallie says. 'She's not been in school for a while.'

'How long is a while?' I ask. I haven't seen her for ages, but I've been deliberately avoiding seeing her, so I'd not thought anything of it.

'A week, maybe?' Naira says. 'She's my deputy on the student council.' Her cheeks flush pink again. 'And she wasn't at the meeting the Thursday before last.'

'I think it's longer,' Gus says. 'Did she miss any meetings before that?'

'It was the first one since the election.' Naira shrugs.

'She sits next to you in English, right?' Hallie asks.

I nod.

'So when was the last time she was there?'

'I've been skipping because I didn't want to see her.' Saying it out loud makes it really hit home how badly I've treated her. 'The last time I went was two or three weeks ago, and she was absent.'

'So she's been gone for around three weeks that we know of,' Naira says. 'And none of us even noticed.'

'We are really bad people,' Gus says. 'No offence.'

None of us say anything because we know he's right. We've been so caught up in our own problems that we haven't thought about how our actions have affected other people. The guilt is so thick around us that I'm surprised we're still breathing.

'So where is she?' Hallie says. 'Is she sick? Has she left school? Or has something worse happened?'

'Worse like what?' Naira says.

'Worse like the Latchitts,' Gus almost whispers it.

'Hold on,' Naira says. 'We're missing something obvious here, because we all feel bad about what we did, but don't you think she's probably in on this?'

'What, like she knows the Latchitts and asked them to punish us?' Gus asks. 'Got herself out of school so she can't be blamed?'

I shake my head. 'No way. There's nothing here that shows she has anything to do with this.'

'Just because there's no proof here, it doesn't mean she's not working with them,' Naira says.

'Naira, you're wrong,' I say. 'I know her. She wouldn't do this.'

'Angelo's a good judge of character,' Hallie says. 'If he says Colette wouldn't be a part of this, then I believe him. And so should you.'

'So where is she then?' Gus says. 'You don't think the Latchitts got to her first, do you?'

I try to think clearly. Work out what we do and don't know. 'There's something that's been bothering me since we first spied on Mrs Latchitt,' I say. 'You know when she threw the chicken down the well?'

They all look at me, waiting to hear what I have to say.

'I don't understand why she did it. I assumed she was feeding the spiders, but that makes no sense as they launched the rest of the chickens on to the field for the spiders to hunt.'

'So why then?' Naira says.

'I think that maybe she was feeding something else,' I say. 'Something we haven't seen yet. Something that can't come to the surface to hunt.'

'Oh my god, they've got Colette trapped in the well,' Hallie gasps, already heading for the door.

'Wait, Hal,' I say. 'We don't know that. Why would they feed a human a live chicken?'

'They're psychos,' Hallie says, turning back for a moment. 'They probably get a kick out of giving her live food and making her kill it with her bare hands. We have to help her. I'm going to the well.'

'Stop, Hal!' I shout, but she's running to the back door like she's just been told she has ten seconds to save the world.

Naira, Gus and I run after her, but we're too far behind. By the time we get to the open door, she's already halfway down the garden.

'Hallie, wait!' Naira yells, but it's like Hallie doesn't even hear. She is laser-focused on that well.

So we run. And despite the pain in my face and chest, despite the ache in every muscle in my body, despite the exhaustion that's been weighing me down since we escaped from the woods, I run faster than I ever have before. I'm gaining ground and just a couple of metres away when Hallie makes it to the well and reaches out to grab the lid, but her hand doesn't even connect with it before something opens it from the inside. I reach for her, thinking I'll have a few seconds to grab her while she tries to lift it. I lunge forward and close my fist around what I expect to be her sleeve, but which turns out to be empty air.

Hallie screams as she's pulled down into the well, and all I see is her feet disappearing into darkness as the lid is yanked shut behind her.

CHAPTER TWENTY

FOUR TO THREE

'No!' Naira gasps as Gus and I slide the lid off and lean into the well. I don't care that it's risky as hell. If Hallie's down there, then I'm going down too.

'Hallie?' I shout, my voice echoing off the walls of the well. I check for a ladder, or some way of climbing down, but there's nothing but smooth rock. I'm a good climber, but I doubt I can get down those surfaces without slipping and falling.

'How do we get down?' Gus asks, looking around us like he might find a magic solution that we didn't notice before.

'I can just drop,' I say. 'If I make it you'll know it's safe, and if I don't . . .'

'Absolutely not, Angelo,' Naira snaps. 'Stop. We can think of a better way.'

But my head and heart are pounding, and I just need to do something. I start to push myself up on to the well.

'No!' Gus grabs the back of my sweatshirt, jerking me towards the ground. He's crying now. 'Please, Angelo, you can't go down there too.'

I feel guilty as I shove him away and make another thrust towards the well.

This time two sets of hands grasp me, pulling me back so violently that I catch my chin on the edge of the well and feel the skin split open, warm blood streaming out. I fall on to the grass, and roll on to my back, using the end of my sleeve to press on the cut. Before I can get up, Naira literally sits on me and pins me down by my shoulders. 'Look at me, Angelo,' she says, trying to make eye contact while I desperately avoid meeting her eyes. 'Look at me!' she shouts. I look at her. 'If we're going to have any chance of getting Hallie back, we need all of us working together. We need a proper plan, and we need your knowledge to make it. Now stop being an idiot.'

So I stop. She's right. Plummeting down a well is not going to help Hallie. 'Sorry,' I say. 'And thanks.'

She nods. Gus slides the lid back over the well. I step away from it and try to get my brain functioning properly.

'We need to get into the tunnels,' I say. 'So we either find a way of getting safely down that well, or we look for another access point.'

'Dude, you're right,' Gus says. 'The Latchitts must have been doing their science stuff somewhere on the school grounds. I mean, all this hasn't happened overnight.'

'So they'd need a place where they're not going to be disturbed, that only they have access to . . .' says Naira. Her braid has come loose – strands of hair blowing around her face. She isn't even bothering to fix it. 'They have the keys to every door in the school.'

'It would have to be somewhere low down, I think, so that the spiders could run around without being seen,' I say.

'They're in the mansion a lot,' says Naira.

'And it has a basement,' I say. 'That must be it. That's where we need to go. But I don't know where the entrance is, and it's going to take too long to search for it, or to find a map.'

'I think I know,' Gus gasps. 'The place where we found Mr Canton's hat when we were looking for him this morning, Naira. Remember it was by that green metal door that I've never seen open before.'

'That's it,' Naira says. 'It must be.'

'So let's go,' Gus says, jogging back towards the cottage.

'Wait,' I say. 'The Latchitts are probably going to be there. And the spiders. They've been a step ahead of us the whole time. If we're going in, we should be prepared.'

'Good idea,' Naira says. 'What exactly are you thinking of?'

'The Latchitts have tools here – things we can use as weapons. We should take what we can – anything that might be useful.'

We raid the cottage and the shed for supplies, filling our pockets and carrying what we can. Gus takes a lighter, and Lady Pointy, who he's taken to talking to a lot. I have a nail gun that I'm both hoping and not hoping to have to use. Naira finds a backpack and stuffs it with anything she can find that could potentially inflict a nasty injury on someone or something. Then we head out of the Latchitts' front door, crunching up the gravel path and out of their gate. We only have a short patch of field to cross, so we stay close together and move fast. We reach the paved area without any disasters, and head towards the mansion.

The front door creaks open when we push it. I worry for a moment that it seems too easy but push that thought away. We step into the wood-panelled entrance room. They've kept it as close to how it was originally as they can, so it feels like we're standing in an old mansion house, and not a school. There's a stag's head watching us from above the door of the head's office – its dead eyes follow us as we tiptoe over flagstones and patterned rugs. Gus leads the way.

We turn left past the office, which I've been 'lucky' enough to see the inside of a couple of times already, and follow the corridor all the way to the end of the building, finally taking a right turn so that we're in the corner closest to the science block. I look at it through the window. It feels like hours since we were sitting on that roof, watching the chickens being picked off one by one. I wonder if that's what will happen to us now.

'Here it is,' Gus whispers, and we stop outside the door. It's old-fashioned so it blends well with its surroundings, even though it's metal rather than wood. Naira reaches forward and grabs the knob, slowly turning it and gently pushing forward. I expect a creak, but unlike every other door in the school, this one moves smoothly and silently. It swings fully open until it rests lightly against the bannister that runs down a flight of stairs into the darkness below.

'It's like it wants us to come in,' Naira says.

We step inside, but don't turn on the light. If there's any chance of getting in without the Latchitts knowing we're coming, we have to take it. But we can't go down the stairs completely blindly, so we turn on a pocket torch we found at the cottage. The beam provides just enough light for us to see three steps ahead, so we follow it in silence, the only sound being our trainers tapping lightly on the smooth stone.

At the bottom we find a small landing, and another metal door.

I turn the knob and start to open it. Light seeps on to the dark landing, so we turn off the torch and push the door slowly, peering through the crack to try to work out what we'll be dealing with before we go running in.

'Oh,' Gus says. 'This is not what I was expecting.'

The huge room in front of us is exactly what you would expect a basement to be. It's a storage room, piled with broken furniture, dusty cardboard boxes and with rolled-up rugs leaning against the walls.

'Maybe we got it wrong,' Naira says, her face falling.

'But I'm sure it's here,' I say. 'And the building above is bigger than this basement room. Let's look behind stuff – see if we can find another door.'

So we stay together, like we promised, and make our way around the room, trying to be methodical and look into every patch of shadow, and behind every grimy piece of furniture.

'What are we looking for, exactly?' Gus whispers. 'A lever that we pull to reveal a secret passage? Like in the movies? Or a bookcase with a trick book that comes out and makes the whole bookcase spin around?'

'It's not *Scooby Doo*, Gus,' I say, although I wish it was. Nothing really bad ever happens in *Scooby Doo*.

'Look,' Naira hisses. 'These piles of stuff look like they've been deliberately placed with gaps in between.' She strides into a gap between two piles, and we follow her round a sort of maze of junk, until we reach another door, set deep into the stone wall.

'OK,' I say, and I'm glad that we've found it, but honestly scared shizless about what we're going to find behind it. I put my hand on the knob.

'Do it,' Gus whispers.

I turn the knob and open the door just a crack. Powerful light seeps out – much brighter and whiter than the yellow glow in the junk room. I hear a regular dripping sound and some faint tapping, but nothing that sounds obviously like the Latchitts. Of course if there are spiders in there, we wouldn't hear them at all.

I push the door and we step into what looks like a science lab. There are high metal benches with clear shining surfaces and empty glass tanks. There are shelves full of clutter – files and equipment piled on top of each other. I notice canisters of pure oxygen lined up against a wall. There's a glass-doored fridge, which is half filled with test tubes and tiny glass phials.

And then there's the wall. The large wall to our right is covered in photos – all overlapping so that they cover it like wallpaper. And they're all of Colette.

'This is even creepier than the board in their cottage,' Gus says, walking over to it.

There are photos of her eating lunch, playing hockey, laughing with a group of friends, laughing with me. There are photos of her making her speech for the student council election, reading in the library, pushing her glasses up because they always slide down her nose. There are derpy faces, happy faces, nervous and sad faces. There's a picture of her face as she confronted me for going through her bag and stealing her money.

'She's not looking into the camera in a single one of them,' I say. 'She didn't know any of these were being taken.'

'Who is she?' Naira asks.

'She's our granddaughter,' a deep male voice says from behind us. We turn to see the Latchitts standing just inside the door, blocking the way out. They're standing there almost casually, like they have no intention of doing anything violent, or creepy, and like they're not at all surprised to find us here.

I think back through every conversation I had with Colette. 'She never mentioned you,' I say. 'She never mentioned having grandparents at all.'

'That's because she doesn't know, sweetling,' Mrs Latchitt says. 'Her mother was our daughter once, but she left us, and hid so we couldn't find her.'

It seems like they're in the mood for talking, so I decide to go with it while I scan the room for escape routes. 'Why did your daughter leave you?'

'Kind of obvious, Angelo,' Gus whispers. 'I mean, you would, wouldn't you?'

'She abandoned us,' Mr Latchitt says. 'Just as our friends and colleagues did.'

'You mean when you were Dr Lachey?' I ask.

'Yes,' Naira says. 'Weren't you well-respected scientists?'

Mrs Latchitt's face lights up. 'We were the best in our field,' she says. 'Everybody said so. We made advances that other people only dreamed about. We took the theories and turned them into reality.'

'Go, Team Lachey,' Gus says.

I can see a door in the wall opposite the one

we came in through. It's the only other way out of this room.

'You have no respect!' Mr Latchitt suddenly shouts – his huge voice filling the room. 'That's the trouble with you, Gustav. You have no respect for anything, or anyone.'

Gus flinches, and for once he doesn't answer back.

'So what happened?' I ask. 'With your friends and colleagues?'

Mrs Latchitt's face hardens. 'They said we went too far. They said the beautiful creatures we were creating were abhorrent and unnatural. We were forced out of the world we loved.'

'But we still had each other.' Mr Latchitt puts his arm around his wife. 'And our grown-up daughter. We loved her as much as we loved our creations.'

'Lucky her,' I say. 'So why did she abandon you?'

'We carried on our work, of course,'

Mr Latchitt says, as if I haven't spoken. 'You can't just walk away from a lifetime of commitment and passion for something.'

'Especially when it's something that could change the course of the world.' Mrs Latchitt smiles again. 'But she didn't like it. That girl.' She spits the words out. 'She didn't agree with what we were doing. She wouldn't let it go.'

'So we realised there was something wrong with her,' says Mr Latchitt, as Mrs Latchitt sways and nods. 'We wanted to help her, but she didn't want to be helped.'

The door on the far wall is different to the others we've come through. It has a handle, not a knob, and an electronic device on one side of it. Towards the bottom of the door there's what looks like a grille, covered by a piece of metal that's fastened over the top.

'One night our little cuckoo fled,' Mrs Latchitt says.

'Disappeared off the face of the earth it seemed,' says Mr Latchitt. 'Of course we weren't going to give up until we found her. It took some time, but eventually we traced her to this town. When the jobs came up at this school, it was perfect, wasn't it?' He smiles at Mrs Latchitt.

'We could continue our work unseen.' She nods so hard I think her neck might break. 'We had access to equipment and all kinds of beautiful beasties who would be the building blocks of our new family.'

'And what a family,' Mr Latchitt says. 'The perfect team of hunters. Loyal to each other, and to us. Deadly, intelligent and easy to train. They became our pack.'

'And we could be close – so very close to our former daughter – without her knowing. We watched her carefully from a distance, hoping to see a change in her – something to show us she repented and wished to return to us. But the only change we saw was her belly swelling as a baby grew inside her. We were sure she would reach out to us then - she would never deprive us of our grandchild. But the months slipped by and we heard nothing. At last we had to accept that she intended to inflict the cruellest wound she could and keep us from our own flesh and blood. We were outside the hospital when she had her baby girl. Our granddaughter. We took pictures as she carried her to the car.' Her face cracks into a full, open-mouthed, toothy grin.

I can't even get my head around how creepy it is.

'And then, lucky for her, Colette ended up coming to this school,' Naira says. I can't see her face, but I'm glad to hear that classic Naira coldness in her voice. She's angry and frustrated, and not afraid.

'It's been the brightest time since we arrived here,' Mr Latchitt says. 'We might have given up on our daughter, but we had something new to hope for. Our Colette, right here where we could keep a close eye on her.'

'And may I say you've done a very thorough

job of that,' Gus says, indicating the photo wall.

'We ensured the school upgraded its security systems,' Mr Latchitt says. 'CCTV covers practically every inch of Dread Wood High. We knew if we watched, and waited, and got to know her from a distance, the day would come when we'd be able to win her for ourselves. Persuade her to join us as a family.'

'So where is she?' I ask and it's like I've flipped a switch.

'SHE'S GONE!' Mrs Latchitt screams, so loud that I instinctively raise my hands to cover my ears.

Mr Latchitt is so angry that he's visibly shaking. 'Because of you,' he says, taking three big strides forward so that he's much closer to us. 'Because of you,' he points at me. 'And you,' he points at Naira. 'And you,' his finger slides to Gus. 'And your hot-headed friend who's currently being prepared for the feeding.'

'You made her cry. You broke her heart.' Mrs

Latchitt is crying now. 'So she left this school, before we had a chance to win her over. Suddenly she was gone, and we lost all hope of having her near.'

It doesn't sit well. It makes me feel like scum. Because it's true, isn't it? A kind, funny, warm person – the only person who's really bothered with me since I started at Dread Wood High, has been made so unhappy that she's quit the school. Because of Naira, and Hallie, and Gus, and maybe a bunch of other people. But mostly because of me. I swear that if we get out of here, I'm going to make things right with her. I think about saying that to the Latchitts – maybe trying to persuade them to let us go so we can get her to come back. But hell no. I'm not begging, and I'm not bargaining with these psychos.

'So what?' I say. 'You decided we should be spider food?'

'Our babies aren't spiders,' Mrs Latchitt says. 'They're so much more than that. After Colette's mother deserted us, we could focus all our love and attention on our adopted children. Aren't they the most beautiful creatures you've ever seen?' She claps her hands. She's absolutely batshiz crazy. 'And today something magical is going to happen.'

'We decided that you should be the ones to play a part in the next stage of their evolution,' Mr Latchitt says. 'We needed to field test them before we move on. And we needed to make sure they had a plentiful food supply to feed their family.'

'Their what, now?' Gus says.

'We're going to be grandparents again!' Mrs Latchitt's eyes shine. 'To hundreds of perfect spiderlings.'

This is so much worse than I thought. And I already thought it was totally freaking terrible.

'What's she talking about, Angelo?' Gus tugs my sleeve like my little brother does when he wants me to explain a TV show.

'You know those giant spider creatures that have spent the last few hours trying to capture, kill or eat us?' I say. 'It looks like they're about to have babies.'

CHAPTER TWENTY-ONE

TICK TOCK

I lift my nail gun, at the same time that Gus raises Lady Pointy, and Naira produces a can of something out of her pocket.

'Where's Hallie?' I ask. 'There are three of us and two of you. You might make it out alive, but you're not going to make it out without taking some serious damage.'

'We'll use these, I swear,' Naira says. 'So just tell us.'

'Oh, sweetlings.' Mrs Latchitt smiles. 'There's no need to wave your toys around like that. We'll tell you where she is.'

'I'm confused,' Gus says.

'Behind that door . . .' Mr Latchitt points at the far wall, 'is a room that leads to a tunnel. Your friend will be in there somewhere. She may or may not still be alive.'

'So show us,' I say, pointing the nail gun at Mrs Latchitt's head. Yeah, I'm angry, but now that I'm in the moment, I realise there's no way I could fire it at a person. The thought of it makes me feel sick.

'Would be delighted to, sweetlings,' Mrs Latchitt says. 'But I'm afraid we need to be on our merry way.'

'No chance.' Naira shakes her head. 'You're a danger to everyone. You need to be in jail.'

'Here's the twist,' Mr Latchitt says. 'You need both Mrs Latchitt and me to open that door. Then you can either go through it, or you can try to stop us from leaving. You won't be able to do both. If you want to save your friend, you'll need to get to her very soon.'

'You're sick,' Gus says.

'Your choice,' Mr Latchitt says.

'Tick tock, tick tock, tick tock,' Mrs Latchitt sings, hopping from one foot to the other with each tick and tock.

But it's not a choice. I don't even need to ask the others what we're going to do.

'Open the door,' I say.

Mr Latchitt walks, and Mrs Latchitt skips over to a computer that's on a bench back by the entrance door. He clicks into a file, and a box appears on the monitor. He enters a password then steps back. Mrs Latchitt enters a second password, pressing the keys slowly, with one finger, and grinning at us the whole time. Then I hear a click from the door at the end of the room.

Naira, Gus and I run to it, and I pull down the handle and push it open. As we step through, I hear Mr Latchitt whistling again, the tune quickly disappearing as they leave through the main door.

Gus swears. Naira swears, which is something you don't get to hear very often. I wonder what the Latchitts' plan is – it feels like we're just a small part of something we don't fully understand. We could be running into a dead end, but I don't think so. This is like a game to them, and it's like they want us to have some kind of spider showdown. So we don't waste time looking back.

In front of us is a rectangular tunnel – man-made from the look of it. It must have been here before the spiders were. It's dimly lit and stretches into darkness, doors going off either side.

'We find Hallie,' I say. 'And we finish this. If those spiderlings get out, the whole town will be overrun in weeks.'

'Hallie first, though?' Gus says, passing Lady Pointy between his hands.

'Hallie first,' I nod.

We run into the tunnel, torch on for all the good it does. I swear I see dark insectoid shapes lurking in every shadow, and I constantly glance upwards, thinking that the tips of hairy legs are brushing the top of my head. From the way both Naira and Gus jump, and swear, I'd say they are thinking the exact same things. I've never been afraid of the dark like lots of kids are, like my little brother is. I'm not one to worry about having my ankles grabbed from under the bed, or half-open wardrobe doors. I know that monsters don't exist. Or at least I did know, before all this.

'Should we check behind the doors?' Gus asks, brushing some imaginary something off his hair.

Each door has an A4-sized sign on it, written in familiar scrawly writing. I get a quick look at them as we run past. One says 'Pack 09: Geospiza . . .' and a load of other Latin-looking words that I don't have time to make out. There's another one that says 'Pack 12: Cestoda . . .' and again, another load of unfamiliar words. If we have a chance later, we need to come back and read them – maybe grab them and take them as evidence.

I feel like they're important.

'I think we're looking for somewhere more natural,' I say. 'Somewhere the spiders have dug out and made their own.'

'A nest, you mean?' Naira asks.

'Yeah,' I say. 'Something like that.'

'Or something like this . . .' Gus stops running and looks in horror at what's in front of us. We've reached the end of the tunnel – or the human part of it at least. The back wall has been cracked open, and there's a large circular passage running off it. It's unlit – totally dark. We can't see where it leads, except that it goes deeper into, and under, the earth. The walls of the tunnel are covered in threads of spider silk, attached around the entrance and then stretching off into the unknown.

'The moment we step into this, they're going to feel us coming,' I whisper. 'Those threads are like a network of tripwires.'

'Any chance of Mission-Impossibling it?' Naira asks.

'Naira,' Gus gasps. 'You used a noun as a verb! Now I know we're all about to die.'

'Everything we touch in that tunnel – every loose piece of soil, every pebble – they'll all be connected to the threads in some way. There's absolutely no chance of us going in unnoticed.' I chew on my lip, thinking. Something's been bothering me all day, and I think it might be something we can use.

'What is it, Angelo?' Naira says. 'You have your thinking face on. It's the same expression you made when we were learning to tell the time in Year 3.'

'I still can't do it without thinking properly hard,' Gus says. 'I hate those oldy-worldy clocks – what a waste of time.' He sniggers and high-fives himself. 'Waste of time!'

'I'm thinking about all the times today when we knew the spiders were close, but they didn't attack the Latchitts,' I say.

'Was it not just because the Latchitts are their creepy-ass parents?' Gus asks.

'That's what I thought,' I say. 'But Mr Latchitt just said something about them being easy to train.'

'So they've been controlling them,' Naira says. 'That makes sense. But how?'

'I think,' I hesitate, just running it through my mind one more time before I say it out loud. 'I think it's the tune. The whistle. I think it stops the spiders from attacking them.'

There's a few seconds of silence, while the others do the sums that I've been trying to work out all day.

'They sang or whistled the tune every time they were outside,' Gus says. 'Walking across the field with the chickens . . .'

'. . . when Mrs Latchitt was at the well,' says Naira.

'And even when Mr Latchitt let us in the gate this morning,' I say. 'We didn't get attacked on the path. They've never come close to us when the Latchitts have been there, singing their little nursery rhyme.'

'And they weren't singing when we were inside their sealed lab,' Gus says. 'But they started again as soon as the doors were open. Angelo! I think you've cracked it!'

'Maybe,' I said. 'I mean, it seems to add up. But we have no way of knowing for sure until we've tested it.'

'And by testing it, you mean . . .' Gus makes a face that suggests he knows exactly what I mean.

'Walking into this tunnel, whistling a kid's song about a spider and a drainpipe, and hoping for the best,' I say.

'You know, as crazy as it sounds, it feels right,' Naira says. 'It makes sense.'

Gus nods. 'We become the Owens.'

'It's still a big risk to take,' I say.

'I trust you, Angelo,' Naira says. 'And I trust us. Together.'

'Also, we don't really have a choice,' Gus says. 'For Hallie!' And he raises Lady Pointy in the air.

'For Hallie,' I nod, tapping my nail gun to Lady Pointy.

'For Hallie.' Naira adds her torch to our salute.

Then we step into the tunnel, me whistling, Naira humming and Gus singing, hoping it will save our lives.

CHAPTER TWENTY-TWO

STALKED

The tunnel is a maze of darkness. The light from our torch illuminates just enough to add shades and depths of black to the walls around us. Every shadow looks like something waiting to pounce. And as we make our way through the earth, our bodies brushing past strands of web, it doesn't take long for the imagined threats to become real ones.

Naira nudges me with her elbow, as a Big Brown-sized shadow creeps across the wall on our left. I adjust my grip on the nail gun, ready to fight if I need to, but I don't stop whistling. As the shape gets close, it hesitates. It's watching us – confused maybe? I'm sure it knows we're not the Latchitts, but if we've got this right then its training should keep it in check for a while at least. It keeps a distance of two or three metres away and backs up the tunnel as we move forward, so it's always just a jump away.

Another twenty paces in, and the dirt wall to our right shifts as we pass. Two inky-black legs feel their way out of a flap of earth I hadn't noticed was there. Another trapdoor. We keep walking, knowing that Red Skull is right behind us.

Every millimetre of my body is on edge, and telling me to either run, or fight. But I keep my pace steady. Keep whistling. We're just starting the second round of 'Incy Wincy', when I feel the slightest touch on my hair. Gus must feel the same, because he yelps, mid-hum, but manages to carry on. I glance up to see a lighter patch on the ceiling, just over our heads. Wolf Grey is skulking along with us.

That's all three, I think. *One in front. One above. One behind.*

It's getting harder to whistle clear and loud. My breath keeps catching, and the notes wobble. I switch to singing, hoping that focusing on the words will help to calm me. I don't think I've ever felt my heart beat so fast, like the momentum of it is going to build and build until it bursts. There's a smell to deal with now too – getting stronger with every step. It's rot, and dried blood, and rancid meat. We had uncooked chicken legs in the fridge at home once, which I was trying to make last, cooking just one each every day for me and my brother. I left them too long and they went bad. The smell was the worst thing to ever hit my nostrils. It stayed in my nose for days after I threw the meat out, and was a painful reminder of what we'd lost. I cried over those wasted chicken legs for weeks. Even now the memory of it makes me furious with myself. And here we are, underground and being stalked by genetically modified giant spiders, and the smell of it is so strong that it's making me gag.

We're in their fridge, I think. And I want to communicate this to the others, but I don't dare stop singing.

I start to see the openings of burrows running off the central one we're walking through. They're smaller – giant spider-sized – and they're all around us. We stick to the main tunnel, heading towards the source of the smell.

We're on to the third round of 'Incy Wincy' when the tunnel ahead of us opens up into a bigger space, like a cavern. The ground underneath us becomes more uneven – littered with stuff that I'm glad I can't see. Something crunches under my foot, and the urge to puke is almost overpowering. I concentrate on staying upright. I do not want to fall over in this filth.

The space in front of us is lighter, somehow. Not lit up, but the edge is being taken off the blackness by something. I look up to see an enormous white mass attached to the roof of the cavern. It's a distorted spherical shape, the size of a small car, and I know exactly what it is, although it's even bigger than I'd imagined. The egg sac. There must be hundreds, if not thousands, of baby spiders inside waiting to hatch and set themselves up with their own burrows and trapdoors. If they get loose, they'll be making their own egg sacs, and that could lead to a full-scale spider apocalypse.

As I edge closer to the sac, my foot catches something and I trip. I instinctively put my hands out to break my fall, dropping the nail gun, and forgetting to keep singing for a second. That second is all the time Wolf needs to drop on to my back as I scrabble in the dirt. She hits me like a freaking bowling ball, my ribs cracking painfully as I wait for the inevitable feel of fangs sinking into my skin. But instead there's a hiss, and the weight lifts as she jumps off. I flip over to see her landing back on the ceiling above, and Gus thrusting his trusty spear at her. I want to thank him, but instead I start singing again.

I scrabble around for my nail gun. I've never shot at anything before, and I don't know if I have it in me to fire at a living creature, but it feels reassuring to have it in my hand. As I feel around in the darkness, I try not to guess what all the squelchy wet stuff is that my fingers keep slipping in. After what feels like ages, but is actually less than a minute, my hand hits the cold, hard plastic, and I pick it up again, then use my other hand to release my foot from whatever it snagged to make me lose my balance. It's a strap of some kind – definitely not spider-made – so I pull at it until it's free from both my foot and the ground goo, and lift it to my face for a proper look. It has a weight to it, and it's clunking about.

Naira squeaks and bends down, moving her hands around whatever it is, until I hear a familiar sound. It's a zip. A zip being zipped. Or unzipped. And then there's light.

It's Mr Canton's bumbag, and our phones are still inside and apparently still functioning. I try not to think about Mr Canton, as I fumble for my rubbish battered phone, with its reassuringly cracked screen. I put the nail gun on my lap as I enter the phone passcode with shaking hands and smile at the sight of my lockscreen glowing gently through the dark. There's no signal down here, which isn't surprising, but there is the torch function. I flick it on and the cavern lights up. It's followed by Gus's and Naira's, and finally we have enough light to give us a chance.

I see loads of stuff all at once: the three spiders shrinking back from the sudden bright light; Mr Canton slumped on the ground to our left; Hallie – or what looks like Hallie – wrapped in spider silk and stuck to the wall on our right, her feet kicking and her eyes and nose just visible; a chicken pecking around in the dirt. God knows how it's still alive – maybe the spiders are saving it for something.

We all run straight to Hallie – sorry, Mr C – and pull at the thread binding her. It's squeezing her tightly, and even with all three of us using all of our strength, we barely move it. We keep singing that godawful tune as Naira takes off her backpack and rummages through one of the pockets, pulling out a knife. She points at herself, mimes a sawing movement towards Hallie, then points at me and on to Mr Canton. I want to help free Hallie, but I can see the sense in what she's saying. Someone needs to check if Mr Canton is alive.

I feel sick as I crunch and squelch over to him. He's ghost-pale, and still bloody from the blow to his head. I reach forward and put my hand to his neck. I've never properly taken a pulse before, but it should be straightforward enough. I mean, it's either there, or it's not.

I really hope it's there.

I feel a flutter under my fingertips, but I can't be sure, so I take them off then try again. Just as I make contact with his freezing-cold skin, he jolts up with a shout, then lies back down again. He's alive, but we need to get him out.

I look over to see Hallie's face emerging from the webbing. She's looking at Naira like she's crazy. 'Naira,' she gasps. But Naira doesn't answer – she just keeps sawing and singing. 'Gus?' She glances down to where Gus is using the point of his spear to try to free her legs. Hallie looks over at me in confusion. I smile and wave, but keep singing. I point at my mouth in an exaggerated way, like I'm playing a shizzy game of charades. Hallie catches on and starts singing too, pulling at the web.

Mr Canton sits up again suddenly, and his eyes focus on my face. 'Angelo?' he says, slurring like he's drunk. 'Why are you singing?' I rub his back and keep going with the song that I know I am going to hate for the rest of my life, however long that might be.

'I know this one.' Mr Canton smiles sleepily. 'Hashtag "Old School".' He starts humming along. I pull him to his feet, just as Hallie drops down from the remains of her sticky prison. She looks good, considering. We all meet in the middle of the cavern, between the sac and the exit. The spiders are still keeping back, away from the song and the light, but always watching.

I grab my phone and start typing. 'Take Mr C back. I'll sort the sac.'

Hallie shakes her head and types: 'No way. I'm staying 2 help.'

'Someone needs to take him,' Naira types. 'He can't get out alone.'

'I'm the only one with a pointy,' Gus writes.

We all glare at each other. I'm not sure why it is that we're all so keen to get ourselves killed, but apparently nobody wants to be the one heading to safety.

'We're wasting time,' I write.

'Fine,' Naira types, and I can hear the huff in it. 'I'll go. I'll prepare the lab for when you get there, and I'll make the trail.' She unzips the backpack again, pulls out a two-litre can of mower fuel, and another can about half the size. 'Use it well,' she types. 'That's all there is.'

She goes to put the bag back over her shoulders when Hallie stops her, puts a hand up signalling for her to wait, then scoops up the chicken and puts it in the bag, zipping it safely inside. Naira rolls her eyes. Then she unscrews the cap on the mower fuel, puts her phone torch in one of Mr Canton's hands and one of her arms around him to support him. She gives us one last smile as they turn and head back down the tunnel, both of them humming, Naira trickling fuel from the can so it splatters on to the ground behind them.

Gus, Hallie and I turn to face the egg sac. In the torchlight from our phones, I can see that it isn't still. It's throbbing and pulsating, and alive with squirming, wriggling creatures underneath the white skin. I place my phone on the ground underneath it, torch light pointing upwards, so that we can see what we're doing well enough while keeping our hands free. *RIP phone*, I think, because I know I probably won't have a chance to take it with me, if we get out of here.

Hallie looks from the phone, to me, then swaps my phone for hers. She types on mine, 'It's my fault we're down here, and my mum will get me a new one.' I smile at her, so grateful, and put mine back in my pocket, glad to hold on to it even if it is old and cracked.

I unscrew the lid on the fuel can, and try to charade out the plan to Hallie, without making it obvious to the spiders. The song has kept them back so far, but even with the best training, I think an assault on their egg sac will tip them over the edge. I'm braced for an attack.

Gus goes back-to-back with me, Lady Pointy

held high, and Hallie stands by my side, holding the knife in one hand and my nail gun in the other.

We step towards the egg sac.

Wolf Grey, Big Brown and Red Skull scuttle behind us like they're itching to go. They know we're up to something, and they don't like it.

We take another step. The egg sac is amazing – the perfect nest for the spiderlings to grow inside. The scale of it is terrifying, though. The writhing young spiders make the skin of it move and stretch in a hundred different places. It looks so close to bursting, and once it does it's game over.

Another step and we're under the sac. I raise the can, the leady smell of the fuel actually a pleasant change from the meat-rot stench. I get ready to squirt and run. And then, as we start another round of 'Incy Wincy', I feel a change in the light around us. A shadow is growing behind the egg sac, looming larger, and blacker, until it fills most of the cavern.

And then a fourth spider – twice the size of the others – drops down in front of us. Its black legs are thick as young tree trunks, and covered with hairs tipped with a copper colour that glints in the light. Like the others it has eight eyes, and nasty-looking fangs underneath them. It rears up on its back legs and comes crashing down on top of us.

This must be Mama.

CHAPTER TWENTY-THREE

LAST GASP

We all dive to avoid being fanged, or trampled, whistling and singing forgotten, but both Hallie and I get caught under its legs. Hallie hacks at a knee with her knife, and it hisses and jumps back a little, giving us just enough time to get to our feet. Gus jabs with his spear, but the other three are circling now. We couldn't beat them before when we had Naira with us too, and this time it's them who outnumber us four to three.

Mama S rears again and I know that we're going to tire of this long before she does.

So I move. As fast as I can, and without stopping to think about how stupid or suicidal it is. I dodge between her two front legs and duck around her, darting from side to side as she tries to impale me on the hooked ends of her feet. I hear Gus and Hallie shouting, trying to distract her. She's bigger than the others, but she's also slower, and I finally get behind her, her body shielding me from being jumped on by the three furious spiders who are scuttling around the edges of the fight. I take my chance and race around the egg sac, sloshing it with fuel as high up as I can get it, so that it drips down the sides and splashes on to the ground.

I hear a roar behind me and turn to see the point of Gus's stick embedded in the spider's abdomen, and Hallie slashing at its eyes with her knife. The giant spider is flailing around, the smaller ones circling, not wanting to get too close to the light, or the fuel, but looking for their opportunity to attack.

'Guys, go,' I shout, shooting back between

Mama's legs to where my friends are fighting for all of our lives. Black slimy liquid sprays out of the spider's eye, covering Hallie.

'This stinks!' Hallie shouts. 'You all freaking stink, you disgusting . . .' she slashes with her knife, 'stinking . . .' she kicks hard with her foot, 'nasty . . .' she slashes again, 'stinkers!'

'Hallie,' I grab her sleeve. 'We need to get out of here.'

Gus gives up trying to pull his stick out of Mama S and reaches into his pocket to grab the lighter.

'Do it, Gus!' I shout.

He flicks it – once, twice, three times. I see Big Brown scurrying across the wall to the left of him, getting ready to jump. He flicks again, the flame catches. Then he drops it.

He swears. We all swear. But some of the fuel that splashed on the ground has ignited. It flares up quickly and spreads to Mama's feet, first taking hold of the places where the liquid has dripped on to her from the egg sac, and then spreading up her legs. She screams.

'Go!' I shout again, and Hallie, Gus and I finally start running for the exit. I turn before we head out, just in time to see the egg sac split open – spiders the size of Frisbees spilling out into the cavern at the same time as the fire takes hold. The egg sac catches, and the air fills with smoke and the stink of burning hair. As I take a step back into the tunnel, I see a burning baby spider curl up and drop to the ground, right where Naira started the fuel trail.

'Run!' I say to the others. 'RUN!'

And we run like never before, injured and exhausted and feeling none of it. The snake of fire starts to slither towards us, getting closer and closer as we pelt up the tunnel, our arms and legs pumping to propel us up the incline. I feel the heat of it behind me. Then we're in the lab tunnel, passing the doors that we'll never get a chance to open now. I see Naira waiting at the lab door – her face wild – she's screaming at us: 'Faster!' The fire catches my ankle, but I don't stop. Hallie is through the door. Gus is just behind her. I'm so close. But something grabs my foot.

I turn to see Big Brown, feet on fire, screaming like a maniac, and holding on tight to my foot. I kick out, trying to ignore the flames creeping up my tracksuit bottoms. Again, and again, and again. It's no good – he has nothing to lose, and he's not letting go.

Then from behind me, someone thumps an oxygen canister down hard on to Big Brown's face. It crunches like cars colliding on the motorway. Big Brown lets go.

'Come on, Angelo.' Naira drops the canister and drags me back by my sweatshirt, so that I'm sliding across the last bit of the tunnel on my ass, looking back at the riot of spider and flames we've left behind. I'm through the door. I kick it shut. Hallie is spraying a fire extinguisher at my leg.

There's a scream from behind the door, and something thuds against it.

'They always come back,' Gus says, grabbing

the nail gun from the floor where Hallie dropped it. 'We've got to finish it.' He lifts the metal flap at the bottom of the door. There's a slotted grill underneath, which Big Brown is trying to pull off with his burning legs. Gus lies on his belly, nail gun in hand, aims and fires.

The shot hits its target as Gus fastens the flap back over the grille and scoots back. There's a sound like a bomb going off behind the door. And the door visibly shakes, buckling slightly.

'Did you just explode the spider?' Naira asks.

'The oxygen canister,' Gus says. 'Just to make sure.'

Smoke starts pouring through the cracks around the door and into the lab.

'That's not going to hold,' I say. 'We need to get out of here.'

So again, we run. Into the basement, slamming the lab door shut behind us. Through the junk maze, shoving broken chairs and boxes of old football kits aside as we plummet across the flagstones. Out to the stairwell, closing the green metal door that we opened so nervously maybe forty minutes ago. Up the stairs. So many stairs. Running even though our bodies are ready to drop. Running like it's the only thing that matters.

We finally reach the top, surfacing into the glorious light and air. Other than the smell of smoke, there's no sign of the fire catching up with us, but I shut the door anyway, hoping that everything we saw under the school will remain there forever. We head towards the entrance hall at a jog, concentrating too hard on breathing to talk.

Mr Canton is sitting on the carpet by the main door, his perfect tracksuit torn and black with dirt. He's still humming 'Incy Wincy Spider'. We get to him just as a police car and ambulance, sirens blaring, come racing up the drive spitting gravel as they go.

'Ah, I remember the words, now,' Mr Canton slurs, grinning like a goofy toddler. '*Then Incy Wincy Spider climbed up the spout again.*'

CHAPTER TWENTY-FOUR

AN END AND A BEGINNING

It's two days since we blew up the school basement, and Dread Wood High is closed while they make sure it's safe for us to be there. The network of tunnels had spread right across the grounds, so sinkholes opened up everywhere. The official line is that the explosion was caused by a gas leak underground. The lab was destroyed, the spiders were incinerated, and the Latchitts disappeared off the face of the earth, so there was no evidence to suggest it was anything else. Of course we told the police what really happened, but even as the words were coming out of our mouths, we knew they wouldn't believe us. The Latchitts left their car and enough of their stuff behind in their house that it all looked totally normal. The police believe they could have died in the explosion, but are still investigating, and Mr Canton can't remember anything that happened, except falling down a hole. At the end of the day, we're a bunch of kids who'd behaved so badly that we'd had to spend a Saturday at school. Our word means nothing.

I get to the Dread Wood, and sit down on the bench that shelters under the biggest horse chestnut tree. It's cold and wet again, but I have a coat and beanie on, and I don't mind at all. Naira arrives next, looking perfect as usual.

'Hey.' She smiles, sitting down next to me.

'Your face is looking better.'

The holes where the spider hairs hit have scabbed over. They're bruising up a bit, but they don't hurt too much.

'Yours too,' I say. 'You must have decided to keep that butt stick out for good.'

'Hey!' She whacks me in the arm.

'What's up?' Gus bowls over like a tiny blond G. He's definitely walking with more swag than before. 'You guys good?'

'Not bad,' Naira says.

'I'm OK,' I say. 'Still mad at you, though.'

'About the mower and the nail gun?' Gus says.

'I've never wanted much in life,' I say. 'But driving that mower and shooting the nail gun were right up there. I didn't get to do either of them.'

'Not my fault I'm a straight savage,' Gus smirks, and sits down next to Naira. 'At least you got to kiss me, Angelo. That's a dream come true for anyone.'

'Sorry I'm late.' Hallie comes running up, carrying two large pizza boxes. 'I brought food.'

'You legend,' Gus says, opening the top box, and then making a face when he sees it's vegetarian.

'What were you hoping for, Gustav?' Hallie grins.

'Something that isn't green,' Gus says. 'But not chicken. Or ham.'

'Cheese feast?' Hallie opens the second box and passes it to me. And we all sit and stuff pizza in our faces in silence for a few minutes.

'How is your chicken?' Gus says, between chews.

'She's doing well, surprisingly,' Hallie says. 'The vet checked her over and couldn't see any major injuries. We had an enclosure built for her in the back garden, with a cute house and a little yard, and she just struts around it like a queen. I'm calling her Michelle.'

'The only chicken survivor of the Dread Wood

High Massacre,' Gus says. 'No wonder she feels like a boss.'

The wind ruffles the grass, and I have to force myself not to stare at the ground, watching for a shift in the earth.

'How long do you think it will take for things to feel normal again?' Naira asks.

'Honestly, I don't think they ever will,' I say.

'Do you think they're watching?' Hallie asks.

We all know who she means. The Latchitts are out there somewhere, and I have a constant sick feeling in the very bottom of my gut that says they're not too far, and that we'll see them again.

'Maybe,' I say. 'But we beat them once. We can do it again if we have to.'

'Club Loser for the win,' Gus cheers.

'I hope we don't have to.' Naira shudders.

'I don't know,' Hallie says. 'It wasn't all bad. I mean good stuff came out of it too.'

We look at each other and smile, and it's almost a beautiful heartfelt moment.

'You mean the jasmine hand cream in the staff toilet,' Gus says. 'If none of this had happened, we would never know of its magical powers to make our hands feel as soft as unicorn fur.'

We all crack up laughing.

'I've asked my mum to get me some,' Gus says. 'I shall no longer have the calloused hands of a man from the wrong side of the tracks.'

'I have a confession to make,' I say.

They all stop laughing and look at me. Concerned.

'It's hard for me to say this, but . . .' I pause. 'I never tried the hand cream.'

'Angelo, what were you thinking?' Gus looks horrified. Hallie and Naira are laughing so hard they can barely breathe.

'It's my one regret from that day,' I say.

'Mine is calling you Ang that time,' Gus says. 'I thought it was a good idea in the moment, but afterwards I just felt like it didn't fit. Like wearing your shoes on the wrong feet.'

We laugh and chat, and finish both pizzas, and then there's no putting it off any longer. We have somewhere to go.

We talk as we walk – stuff about how our parents are dealing with what happened to us, wondering when school will be open again. But when we arrive at the gate, we fall completely silent. I feel sick with nerves. I've been thinking about this moment non-stop since our detention. I've played it out in my mind. All the different ways it could go. The ways I could mess it up. The ways I could do it right. I look at the others and I'm guessing they're feeling the same way I do, but I think, out of all of us, it means the most to me. I have more to lose.

We look at each other and push open the gate. I lead the way up the path and step up to the door. I glance around once more and they all nod. We're ready for this. I ring the bell.

Colette Huxley opens the door, looking just as she did the last time I saw her. Her honey-coloured hair is twisted up in a complicated-looking situation, with tiny silk daisies poked in random places. Her brown eyes stare at me like she doesn't know what to make of me, and her expression is a mix of surprise and hurt. Then she notices the others behind me and takes a small step back, like she's flinching away from us.

'Hi, Colette,' I say. 'I know you have no reason to want to talk to any of us, and honestly we wouldn't blame you if you slammed the door in our faces.'

She doesn't say anything, just watches in confusion as I try to string my sentences together.

'We're here because of what we did to you,' I say. 'We want to make things right. I want to make things right.'

She hesitates, then steps back, opening the door wider. 'Do you want to come in? It's freezing.'

'I think we'd all really love that,' I say,

struggling to keep tears out of my eyes.

We follow her through her house and into her conservatory. We sit on comfy sofas, and she sits on a chair, watching us.

'I'm listening,' she says.

Rain patters down on the glass above our heads, and it calms me. Helps me to slow my pounding heart. I have so much I need to say to her, but there's only one place to start.

'Colette, I am so sorry.'

She blinks. A tear slides down her cheek and spatters on her jeans. Then she pushes her glasses up her nose and smiles. It's a small smile, not her usual goofy grin, but it's genuine. I'll take it.

So we talk, and we listen. As the hours pass, the rain keeps drumming on the glass walls around us, never letting up. Outside, I see the tops of the tallest trees in the Dread Wood, looming silently as always. But inside, things are changing. Two days ago, I was alone. Fighting battles with my back against the wall.

Angry at the world and even angrier at myself. But I realise that somewhere along the way, at some unknown point in the detention from hell, I made a choice. I chose to own my mistakes. I chose to repair the damage I'd caused. I chose to move forward, not alone, but with people I trust at my back. My friends. My pack.

FLINCH:
A PLAYER'S GUIDE

Turn fear into fun with 'Flinch' - the most exciting game you'll ever play. Earn points by scaring your friends in this brand new, fast-paced, thrill-fest of a game that is taking the world by storm. Don't miss out - download the FREE Flinch app now and scare your way to victory.

Once the app is downloaded, you will be assigned a unique player reference. From that moment on, you are part of the game and, should your app alert you of the start of a round, you MUST play.

The Flinch app selects players using geographical location – being in an area where a large number of players are collected increases the chances of a round being announced. Players will be notified of the start of a round by the Flinch tune playing on their mobile devices. The Flinch tune is 'Pop Goes The Weasel', a nursery rhyme used in traditional jack-in-the-box toys. Imagine turning the handle on the box, winding it slowly towards a jump-scare. Players have until the music stops to take their places, ready to play. When the first part of the Flinch tune stops playing, there will be a random and undetermined number of minutes for gameplay, during which players must try to score as many points as possible. The round will end when the final line of the Flinch tune plays and the final jump-scare has popped.

During game play, the rules are simple:

The aim is to make other players flinch. A flinch is a physical reaction to a scare – a gasp, a jump, a shout, or running away.

1. A flinch can be obtained through any means, except physical contact. No touching.

2. When a flinch is obtained, the flincher must use the app to give a point to the player who scared them, simply by holding their mobile devices close together and clicking a button.

Failure to follow the rules will result in player elimination. The players with the most points will be rewarded with a coveted place on the Flinch leaderboard.

Do you have what it takes to scare your way to the top? There's only one way to find out . . .

CHAPTER ONE

THE GAME

A scream splits the silence of the Dread Wood. I brace myself against the tree behind me and force myself to be still. Not easy when my body feels like a human beehive. Under my skin everything is buzzing, vibrating, like I might explode at any moment, splattering blood and body parts across the green of the woods. I picture it for a second, and strangely enough the thought distracts me enough to calm me. The image leaves me with one lasting thought: I do not want to die at this school.

Quiet again. Time to move. I can't resist a quick glance above me and a scan of the ground ahead. The memory of the last time I was hunted in these woods will always be with me, but I remind myself that the spiders are gone. I'm facing a different enemy now – fewer legs but almost as frightening.

I dart forward, keeping in the shadows as much as I can, avoiding the bright sunlight that streaks through the gaps between the trees. I reckon I know these woods better than most people, which gives me an advantage. There are places where I know people will be hiding – the hollowed-out bushes close to the paths, which make everyone who finds them think they've discovered some massive secret, until they spot the screwed-up sweet wrappers and left-behind drink bottles. Someone will be huddling in there now, thinking they have the drop on whoever passes by. Easy target.

As I get close to one of the hollows, I see movement. It's too early in spring for everything in the woods to have properly filled out – shrubs are still budding, leaves uncurling. Through the tiny shoots of green, I can see a dark shape, crouching, shifting slightly on their feet like they can't keep still.

I hold back for a moment before I make my move. It could be a trap – someone acting as bait while an ally waits to pounce. That's the trouble with Flinch: you're never sure whether you're the hunter or the prey.

In the second before I attack, I hear something that stops me in my tracks. A squeak of fright and then a hiss of disgust as whoever it is brushes a bug off the sleeve of their sweatshirt.

'Naira,' I say. 'You're lucky it's me who found you first, otherwise you'd be flinched for sure.'

'Oh god, Angelo.' Naira looks out at me and holds up a hand for me to help her out of the hollow. 'This bush is infested. Did you see that disgusting creature? What was it?'

'A beetle, I think.' I pull her under a branch and out into the open. 'It was hard to tell, what with you being in a shadowy bush, and the creature being only a few millimetres long.'

'Small doesn't mean harmless,' Naira huffs, brushing invisible bugs off her PE kit. 'Just look at Hallie.'

I grin. 'We need to get out of here. Game's not over yet.'

'I'm coming with you,' Naira says, retying her ponytail. 'And don't look at me like that – I'd be perfect on my own, anywhere but in these woods.'

I nod, but I'm already looking forward to telling the others about this later and seeing the glare on her face. 'Let's go.' I lead her away from the path. She's strong, fast, and stealthy, and I'm glad to have her at my back.

We jog further into the Dread Wood, only stopping now and again to look, and to listen.

Nobody knows exactly when Flinch became a thing, or who played the first game. We started hearing about it a few weeks ago, through listening in on muttered chats in the dining hall, between clustered groups of people hunched over pizza slices. Once it started being talked about in all the usual places online, there wasn't a person in the school who didn't know what it was or how to play. Everyone has the Flinch app, and once you have the app, it's impossible to resist joining in. Even for me, and I'm usually really good at resisting joining in with stuff.

The rules are simple. The Flinch app notifies players at the start of a round by playing the start of a tune – *'Half a pound of tuppenny rice, half a pound of treacle, that's the way the money goes . . .'* In that time everyone scatters, hides, finds places to launch their attacks from. The aim is to make other players flinch or run away, usually by jump-scaring them, but everyone has their own technique. Physical contact isn't allowed, but other than that, anything is fair game. If you make someone flinch you connect the Flinch apps on your phones to claim your point. The round ends when the app plays the end of the song.

'Do you have a plan?' Naira whispers. 'Surely nobody's going to be hiding this far in? I want to win, not get lost so deep in the woods that my body isn't located until I've been eaten by maggots.'

'We're going to circle back,' I say. 'I know another noob spot we can check out – bound to be someone lurking in there.'

'Well, can we circle back soon? The round's going to end, I have won zero flinches today, and I'm starting to feel like I'm in the Hunger Games, out here in all this nature.'

'Any sign of the others?' I spot the boundary fence through the trees – the place where the school grounds end but the Dread Wood goes on, past the train tracks, until it reaches the edge of town.

'If Hallie was close, I feel like I would have known instantly, so she must be over the other side of the woods . . .' Naira says. I nod – Hallie's game tactics involve less sneaking in for surprise attacks, and more shouting aggressively at people until they can't stand it any more and give her the Flinch point. 'I heard a scream about five minutes ago that I'm pretty sure was Gus,' Nai carries on. 'I mean the pitch of it – how he sounds like a stepped-on puppy – it's distinct, you know?'

'It is,' I say. I hesitate, but I have to ask. 'What about Colette?'

I'm glad Naira is behind me so she can't see my cheeks burning. I know she knows anyway – I can picture her annoying expression, just like she can picture mine.

'I have no idea about Colette,' she says. 'You know how she is – for someone so apparently pure of heart, she's incredibly good at sneaking.'

It's true that Colette is a lot of things all at once – I've never known anyone like her. Naira, Gus, Hallie, and me were forced together following a Saturday detention that turned into a fight for our lives. Looking back, it feels impossible, even to us, that we were hunted by genetically mutated giant spiders. Impossible, insane, unreal. But it happened.

Experiences like that make you bond with people – you have to if you're going to make it out with your body and mind intact. In one day we went from being people who didn't even look at each other in the corridor to good friends. Over the past three months we've grown even closer, but there's still a lot we don't know about each other.

With Colette, things are even more complicated. The rest of us were in detention that day because we treated her badly. Worse than badly. We were awful to her. Once detention was over, all we wanted to do was apologise. I never expected to be forgiven, but Colette being Colette, I was. We all were. And since then we've all stuck together. Being part of a group is new for me – feels as uncertain as walking across the school field, wondering if there's something lying in wait under the ground. Like a trapdoor could open up under my feet.

Something stops me, suddenly. I don't know if I saw some movement in the corner of my eye, or picked up the smallest sound or if it was just a feeling – nothing specific, but my body tenses. I put a hand on Naira's shoulder, turn and meet her eyes, trying to warn her without speaking. I don't know if she senses it too, or if she gets my message loud and clear, but she freezes instantly. We stand shoulder-to-shoulder, not even breathing, watching the woods around us. The bees inside me thrum quietly, stingers ready. My whole body knows it: we're being watched.

'Where?' Naira says.

'Not sure,' I say. 'Behind, to the left, maybe. I think there's someone there.'

I'm too focused, too alert. My eyes are staring so hard that they're blurring. All I see are tree trunks, every one different but at the same time somehow the same: murky, towering, twisting pillars, concealing a million things. I try to relax and breathe in through my nose – the moss and earth scent of the woods always soothes me – but I can't smell anything except the sting inside my nose as it sucks in the chill, damp air. The back of my neck is itching, and it takes everything in me not to scratch it like a bear against a tree trunk. I stare into the Dread Wood as branches creak and sway in the breeze. Maybe I can see the start of a silhouette behind a cluster of evergreens, but I could be imagining it.

It's Naira who snaps me out of it. 'We should move,' she whispers. 'If there's someone there, they're going to follow, and then we'll know.'

I nod. We turn and walk on.

A twig snaps behind us, and my heart lurches. I feel Naira tense up, but we keep moving as if we haven't heard it. The best thing we can do is lure them in, so when the ambush comes we're ready for it. I remind myself that it doesn't matter if someone jumps out, only that we stay strong and don't flinch . . .

ACKNOWLEDGEMENTS

Starting a new job is scary, but it's been such a pleasure and privilege to work with Farshore on this book. The most enormous thanks go to Sarah Levison and Lindsey Heaven for taking a chance on me and giving me the confidence to write a story that I love. I couldn't ask for a more lovely or brilliant editor than Sarah. Thanks also to Lucy Courtenay and Melissa Hyder, who made this book LOADS better. I love how *Dread Wood* looks, and that is thanks to the illustrating talents of Tom Clohosy Cole and design brilliance from Ryan Hammond. I'm hugely grateful to the PR and Marketing teams, especially Hannah, Olivia and Samara, who have worked hard to help my story fly.

I'm incredibly grateful to my wonderful agent, Kirsty McLachlan, who has supported, boosted and advised me with such kindness and wisdom over the last four years. I'm so lucky to have her with me.

I wouldn't be writing the acknowledgements for my seventh book without the support of a lot of people. Heartfelt thanks go to every teacher, TA, librarian, blogger and bookseller who has championed my books. I'm also lucky to have the loveliest friends, both old and new – I hope you know how grateful I am to have you in my life. I have to say a special thank you to Eloise Williams, Les Hall and Lorraine Gregory, who have supported me through a particularly tough year.

Thanks to Mum, Dad, Julie and Alfie for having my back and trying to sell my books to anyone who'll listen. And thanks to my chaotic, hilarious, brilliant and loving family – Dean, Mia, Stanley, Helena, Luis and Teddy – for being the lights of my life and my best friends.

Much of Dread Wood High is based on my old high school, Bishopshalt, and I owe a huge thank you to Mr McGillicuddy and Mrs Bermingham, who generously allowed me to visit last year and retrace my teenage steps through still familiar corridors and pathways. Those who know Bishopshalt will no doubt recognise many features in the buildings and grounds of Dread Wood High, but rest assured that the people and events of the story have been created entirely in my twisted imagination. I never attended a Saturday detention at Bishopshalt, but I have been informed that nothing even remotely dangerous ever happened!

And of course, thank you to every wonderful reader. Welcome to Club Loser – I hope you have an unforgettable adventure.

JENNIFER KILLICK

Jennifer Killick is the author of *Crater Lake, Crater Lake, Evolution* and the *Alex Sparrow* series. Jennifer regularly visits schools and festivals, and her books have been selected four times for the Reading Agency's Summer Reading Challenge. She lives in Uxbridge, in a house full of children, animals and books. When she isn't busy mothering or step-mothering (which isn't often) she loves to watch scary movies and run as fast as she can, so she is fully prepared for witches, demons, and the zombie apocalypse.